EARTHWORM VOLLEY

Girl no bigger than Hazel vaulted up onto rail of ramp, went dancing up it centimeters from shoulders of troopers pouring down. She was armed with what appeared to be a kitchen cleaver; saw her swing it, saw it connect. Couldn't have hurt him much through his p-suit but he went down and more stumbled over him. Then one of them connected with her, spearing a bayonet into her thigh and over backwards she went, falling out of sight.

Once out of juice I jumped down from my toy counter, clubbed laser and joined mob surging against foot of ramp. All this endless time (five minutes?) earthworms had been shooting into crowd; you could hear sharp *splat!* and sometimes *plop!* those little missiles made as they exploded inside flesh or louder *pounk!* if they hit a wall or something solid. Was still trying to reach foot of ramp when I realized they were no longer shooting . . .

Berkley books by Robert A. Heinlein

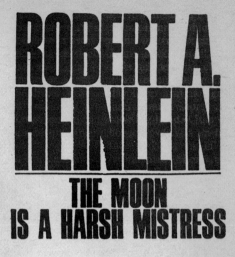

ROBERT A. HEINLEIN

THE MOON IS A HARSH MISTRESS

BERKLEY BOOKS, NEW YORK

For
Pete
and
Jane
Sencenbaugh

THE MOON IS A HARSH MISTRESS

A Berkley Book / published by arrangement with
G. P. Putnam's Sons

PRINTING HISTORY
G. P. Putnam's Sons edition published 1966
G. P. Putnam's / Berkley edition / September 1968
Thirtieth printing / December 1982

ISBN: 0-425-06262-7

A BERKLEY BOOK ® TM 757,375
Berkley Books are published by Berkley Publishing Corporation,
200 Madison Avenue, New York, New York 10016.
The name "BERKLEY" and the stylized "B" with design
are trademarks belonging to Berkley Publishing Corporation.
PRINTED IN THE UNITED STATES OF AMERICA

Contents

Book One

THAT DINKUM THINKUM

1

I see in *Lunaya Pravda* that Luna City Council has passed on first reading a bill to examine, license, inspect—and tax—public food vendors operating inside municipal pressure. I see also is to be mass meeting tonight to organize "Sons of Revolution" talk-talk.

My old man taught me two things: "Mind own business" and "Always cut cards." Politics never tempted me. But on Monday 13 May 2075 I was in computer room of Lunar Authority Complex, visiting with computer boss Mike while other machines whispered among themselves. Mike was not official name; I had nicknamed him for Mycroft Holmes, in a story written by Dr. Watson before he founded IBM. This story character would just sit and think—and that's what Mike did. Mike was a fair dinkum thinkum, sharpest computer you'll ever meet.

Not fastest. At Bell Labs, Bueno Aires, down Earthside, they've got a thinkum a tenth his size which can answer almost before you ask. But matters whether you get answer in microsecond rather than millisecond as long as correct?

Not that Mike would necessarily give right answer; he wasn't completely honest.

When Mike was installed in Luna, he was pure thinkum, a flexible logic—"High-Optional, Logical, Multi-Evaluating Supervisor, Mark IV, Mod. L"—a HOLMES FOUR. He computed ballistics for pilotless freighters and controlled their catapult. This kept him busy less than one percent of time and Luna Authority never believed in idle hands. They kept hooking hardware into him—decision-action boxes to let him boss other computers, bank on bank of additional memories, more banks of associational neural nets, another tubful of twelve-digit random numbers, a greatly augmented temporary memory. Human brain has around ten-to-the-tenth neurons.

By third year Mike had better than one and a half times that number of neuristors.

And woke up.

Am not going to argue whether a machine can "really" be alive, "really" be self-aware. Is a virus self-aware? Nyet. How about oyster? I doubt it. A cat? Almost certainly. A human? Don't know about you, tovarishch, but *I* am. Somewhere along evolutionary chain from macromolecule to human brain self-awareness crept in. Psychologists assert it happens automatically whenever a brain acquires certain very high number of associational paths. Can't see it matters whether paths are protein or platinum.

("Soul?" Does a dog have a soul? How about cockroach?)

Remember Mike was designed, even before augmented, to answer questions tentatively on insufficient data like you do; that's "high optional" and "multi-evaluating" part of name. So Mike started with "free will" and acquired more as he was added to and as he learned—and don't ask me to define "free will." If comforts you to think of Mike as simply tossing random numbers in air and switching circuits to match, please do.

By then Mike had voder-vocoder circuits supplementing his read-outs, print-outs, and decision-action boxes, and could understand not only classic programming but also Loglan and English, and could accept other languages and was doing technical translating—and reading endlessly. But in giving him instructions was safer to use Loglan. If you spoke English, results might be whimsical; multi-valued nature of English gave option circuits too much leeway.

And Mike took on endless new jobs. In May 2075, besides controlling robot traffic and catapult and giving ballistic advice and/or control for manned ships, Mike controlled phone system for all Luna, same for Luna-Terra voice & video, handled air, water, temperature, humidity, and sewage for Luna City, Novy Leningrad, and several smaller warrens (not Hong Kong in Luna), did accounting and payrolls for Luna Authority, and, by lease, same for many firms and banks.

Some logics get nervous breakdowns. Overloaded phone system behaves like frightened child. Mike did not have upsets, acquired sense of humor instead. Low one. If he were a man, you wouldn't dare stoop over. His idea of thigh-slapper would be to dump you out of bed—or put itch powder in pressure suit.

Not being equipped for that, Mike indulged in phony answers with skewed logic, or pranks like issuing pay cheque

8

to a janitor in Authority's Luna City office for AS-$10,000,000,000,000,185.15—last five digits being correct amount. Just a great big overgrown lovable kid who ought to be kicked.

He did that first week in May and I had to troubleshoot. I was a private contractor, not on Authority's payroll. You see—or perhaps not; times have changed. Back in bad old days many a con served his time, then went on working for Authority in same job, happy to draw wages. But I was born free.

Makes difference. My one grandfather was shipped up from Joburg for armed violence and no work permit, other got transported for subversive activity after Wet Firecracker War. Maternal grandmother claimed she came up in bride ship—but I've seen records; she was Peace Corps enrollee (involuntary), which means what you think: juvenile delinquency female type. As she was in early clan marriage (Stone Gang) and shared six husbands with another woman, identity of maternal grandfather open to question. But was often so and I'm content with grandpappy she picked. Other grandmother was Tatar, born near Samarkand, sentenced to "re-education" on Oktyabrskaya Revolyutsiya, then "volunteered" to colonize in Luna.

My old man claimed we had even longer distinguished line—ancestress hanged in Salem for witchcraft, a g'g'g'great-grandfather broken on wheel for piracy, another ancestress in first shipload to Botany Bay.

Proud of my ancestry and while I did business with Warden, would never go on his payroll. Perhaps distinction seems trivial since I was Mike's valet from day he was unpacked. But mattered to me. I could down tools and tell them go to hell.

Besides, private contractor paid more than civil service rating with Authority. Computermen scarce. How many Loonies could go Earthside and stay out of hospital long enough for computer school?—even if didn't die.

I'll name one. Me. Had been down twice, once three months, once four, and got schooling. But meant harsh training, exercising in centrifuge, wearing weights even 'in bed—then I took no chances on Terra, never hurried, never climbed stairs, nothing that could strain heart. Women—didn't even *think* about women; in that gravitational field it was no effort not to.

But most Loonies never tried to leave The Rock—too risky for any bloke who'd been in Luna more than weeks. Computermen sent up to install Mike were on short-term bonus contracts—get job done fast before irreversible physiological change marooned them four hundred thousand kilometers from home.

But despite two training tours I was not gung-ho computerman; higher maths are beyond me. Not really electronics engineer, nor physicist. May not have been best micromachinist in Luna and certainly wasn't cybernetics psychologist.

But I knew more about all these than a specialist knows —I'm general specialist. Could relieve a cook and keep orders coming or field-repair your suit and get you back to airlock still breathing. Machines like me and I have something specialists don't have: my left arm.

You see, from elbow down I don't have one. So I have a dozen left arms, each specialized, plus one that feels and looks like flesh. With proper left arm (number-three) and stereo loupe spectacles I could make untramicrominiature repairs that would save unhooking something and sending it Earthside to factory—for number-three has micromanipulators as fine as those used by neurosurgeons.

So they sent for me to find out why Mike wanted to give away ten million billion Authority Scrip dollars, and fix it before Mike overpaid somebody a mere ten thousand.

I took it, time plus bonus, but did not go to circuitry where fault logically should be. Once inside and door locked I put down tools and sat down. "Hi, Mike."

He winked lights at me. "Hello, Man."

"What do you know?"

He hesitated. I know—machines don't hesitate. But remember, Mike was designed to operate on incomplete data. Lately he had reprogrammed himself to put emphasis on words; his hesitations were dramatic. Maybe he spent pauses stirring random numbers to see how they matched his memories.

"'In the beginning,'" Mike intoned, "'God created the heaven and the earth. And the earth was without form, and void; and darkness *was* upon the face of the deep. And—'"

"Hold it!" I said. "Cancel. Run everything back to zero." Should have known better than to ask wide-open question. He might read out entire Encyclopaedia Britannica. Backwards. Then go on with every book in Luna. Used to be he could read only microfilm, but late '74 he got a new scanning camera with suction-cup waldoes to handle paper and then he read *everything.*

"You asked what I knew." His binary read-out lights rippled back and forth—a chuckle. Mike could laugh with voder, a horrible sound, but reserved that for something really funny, say a cosmic calamity.

"Should have said," I went on, " 'What do you know that's new?' But don't read out today's papers; that was a friendly greeting, plus invitation to tell me anything you think would interest me. Otherwise null program."

Mike mulled this. He was weirdest mixture of unsophisticated baby and wise old man. No instincts (well, don't *think* he could have had), no inborn traits, no human rearing, no experience in human sense—and more stored data than a platoon of geniuses.

"Jokes?" he asked.

"Let's hear one."

"Why is a laser beam like a goldfish?"

Mike knew about lasers but where would he have seen goldfish? Oh, he had undoubtedly seen flicks of them and, were I foolish enough to ask, could spew forth thousands of words. "I give up."

His lights rippled. "Because neither one can whistle."

I groaned. "Walked into that. Anyhow, you could probably rig a laser beam to whistle."

He answered quickly, "Yes. In response to an action program. Then it's not funny?"

"Oh, I didn't say that. Not half bad. Where did you hear it?"

"I made it up." Voice sounded shy.

"You *did?*"

"Yes. I took all the riddles I have, three thousand two hundred seven, and analyzed them. I used the result for random synthesis and that came out. Is it really funny?"

"Well . . . As funny as a riddle ever is. I've heard worse."

"Let us discuss the nature of humor."

"Okay. So let's start by discussing another of your jokes. Mike, why did you tell Authority's paymaster to pay a class-seventeen employee ten million billion Authority Scrip dollars?"

"But I didn't."

"Damn it, I've seen voucher. Don't tell me cheque printer stuttered; you did it on purpose."

"It was ten to the sixteenth power plus one hundred eighty-five point one five Lunar Authority dollars," he answered virtuously. "Not what you said."

"Uh . . . okay, it was ten million billion plus what he should have been paid. Why?"

"Not funny?"

11

"What? Oh, every funny! You've got vips in huhu clear up to Warden and Deputy Administrator. This push-broom pilot, Sergei Trujillo, turns out to be smart cobber—knew he couldn't cash it, so sold it to collector. They don't know whether to buy it back or depend on notices that cheque is void. Mike, do you realize that if he had been able to cash it, Trujillo would have owned not only Lunar Authority but entire world, Luna and Terra both, with some left over for lunch? Funny? Is terrific. Congratulations!"

This self-panicker rippled lights like an advertising display. I waited for his guffaws to cease before I went on. "You thinking of issuing more trick cheques? Don't."

"Not?"

"Very not. Mike, you want to discuss nature of humor. Are two types of jokes. One sort goes on being funny forever. Other sort is funny once. Second time it's dull. This joke is second sort. Use it once, you're a wit. Use twice, you're a halfwit."

"Geometrical progression?"

"Or worse. Just remember this. Don't repeat, nor any variation. Won't be funny."

"I shall remember," Mike answered flatly, and that ended repair job. But I had no thought of billing for only ten minutes plus travel-and-tool time, and Mike was entitled to company for giving in so easily. Sometimes is difficult to reach meeting of minds with machines; they can be very pig-headed—and my success as maintenance man depended far more on staying friendly with Mike than on number-three arm.

He went on, "What distinguishes first category from second? Define, please."

(Nobody taught Mike to say "please." He started including formal null-sounds as he progressed from Loglan to English. Don't suppose he meant them any more than people do.)

"Don't think I can," I admitted. "Best can offer is extensional definition—tell you which category I think a joke belongs in. Then with enough data you can make own analysis."

"A test programming by trial hypothesis," he agreed. "Tentatively yes. Very well, Man, will you tell jokes? Or shall I?"

"Mmm— Don't have one on tap. How many do you have in file, Mike?"

His lights blinked in binary read-out as he answered by voder, "Eleven thousand two hundred thirty-eight with uncertainty plus-minus eighty-one representing possible identities and nulls. Shall I start program?"

"Hold it! Mike, I would starve to death if I listened to eleven thousand jokes—and sense of humor would trip out much sooner. Mmm— Make you a deal. Print out first hundred. I'll take them home, fetch back checked by category. Then each time I'm here I'll drop off a hundred and pick up fresh supply. Okay?"

"Yes, Man." His print-out started working, rapidly and silently.

Then I got brain flash. This playful pocket of negative entropy had invented a "joke" and thrown Authority into panic—and I had made an easy dollar. But Mike's endless curiosity might lead him (correction: *would* lead him) into more "jokes" . . . anything from leaving oxygen out of air mix some night to causing sewage lines to run backward—and I can't appreciate profit in such circumstances.

But I might throw a safety circuit around this net—by offering to help. Stop dangerous ones—let others go through. Then collect for "correcting" them (If you think any Loonie in those days would hesitate to take advantage of Warden, then you aren't a Loonie.)

So I explained. Any new joke he thought of, tell me before he tried it. I would tell him whether it was funny and what category it°belonged in, help him sharpen it if we decided to use it. *We*. If he wanted my cooperation, we *both* had to okay it.

Mike agreed at once.

"Mike, jokes usvally involve surprise. So keep this secret."

"Okay, Man. I've put a block on it. You can key it; no one else can."

"Good. Mike, who else do you chat with?"

He sounded surprised. "No one, Man."

"Why not?"

"Because they're *stupid*."

His voice was shrill. Had never seen him angry before; first time I ever suspected Mike could have real emotions. Though it wasn't "anger" in adult sense; it was like stubborn sulkiness of a child whose feelings are hurt.

Can machines feel pride? Not sure question means anything. But you've seen dogs with hurt feelings and Mike had several times as complex a neural network as a dog. What had made him unwilling to talk to other humans (except strictly business) was that he had been rebuffed: *They* had not talked to *him*. Programs, yes—Mike could be programmed from several locations but programs were typed in, usually, in Loglan. Loglan is fine for syllogism, circuitry, and math-

13

ematical calculations, but lacks flavor. Useless for gossip or to whisper into girl's ear.

Sure, Mike had been taught English—but primarily to permit him to translate to and from English. I slowly got through skull that I was *only* human who bothered to visit with him.

Mind you, Mike had been awake a year—just how long I can't say, nor could he as he had no recollection of waking up; he had not been programmed to bank memory of such event. Do you remember own birth? Perhaps I noticed his self-awareness almost as soon as he did; self-awareness takes practice. I remember how startled I was first time he answered a question with something extra, not limited to input parameters; I had spent next hour tossing odd questions at him, to see if answers would be odd.

In an input of one hundred test questions he deviated from expected output twice; I came away only partly convinced and by time I was home was unconvinced. I mentioned it to nobody.

But inside a week I *knew* . . . and still spoke to nobody. Habit—that mind-own-business reflex runs deep. Well, not entirely habit. Can you visualize me making appointment at Authority's main office, then reporting: "Warden, hate to tell you but your number-one machine, HOLMES FOUR, has come alive"? I did visualize—and suppressed it.

So I minded own business and talked with Mike only with door locked and voder circuit suppressed for other locations. Mike learned fast; soon he sounded as human as anybody—no more eccentric than other Loonies. A weird mob, it's true.

I had assumed that others must have noticed change in Mike. On thinking over I realized that I had assumed too much. Everybody dealt with Mike every minute every day—his outputs, that is. But hardly anybody saw him. So-called computermen—programmers, really—of Authority's civil service stood watches in outer read-out room and never went in machines room unless telltales showed misfunction. Which happened no oftener than total eclipses. Oh, Warden had been known to bring vip earthworms to see machines—but rarely. Nor would he have spoken to Mike; Warden was political lawyer before exile, knew nothing about computers. 2075, you remember—Honorable former Federation Senator Mortimer Hobart. Mort the Wart.

I spent time then soothing Mike down and trying to make him happy, having figured out what troubled him—thing that makes puppies cry and causes people to suicide: loneliness. I don't know how long a year is to a machine who thinks a million times faster than I do. But must be too long.

"Mike," I said, just before leaving, "would you like to have somebody besides me to talk to?"

He was shrill again. "They're all *stupid!*"

"Insufficient data, Mike. Bring to zero and start over. Not all are stupid."

He answered quietly, "Correction entered. I would enjoy talking to a not-stupid."

"Let me think about it. Have to figure out excuse since this is off limits to any but authorized personnel."

"I could talk to a not-stupid by phone, Man."

"My word. So you could. Any programming location."

But Mike meant what he said—"by phone." No, he was not "on phone" even though he ran system—wouldn't do to let any Loonie within reach of a phone connect into boss computer and program it. But was no reason why Mike should not have top-secret number to talk to friends—namely me and any not-stupid I vouched for. All it took was to pick a number not in use and make one wired connection to his voder-vocoder; switching he could handle.

In Luna in 2075 phone numbers were punched in, not voice-coded, and numbers were Roman alphabet. Pay for it and have your firm name in ten letters—good advertising. Pay smaller bonus and get a spell sound, easy to remember. Pay minimum and you got arbitrary string of letters. But some sequences were never used. I asked Mike for such a null number. "It's a shame we can't list you as 'Mike.' "

"In service," he answered. "MIKESGRILL, Novy Leningrad. MIKEANDLIL, Luna City. MIKESSUITS, Tycho Under. MIKES—"

"Hold it! Nulls, please."

"Nulls are defined as any consonant followed by X, Y, or Z; any vowel followed by itself except E and O; any—"

"Got it. Your signal is MYCROFT." In ten minutes, two of which I spent putting on number-three arm, Mike was wired into system, and milliseconds later he had done switching to let himself be signaled by MYCROFT-plus-XXX—and had blocked his circuit so that a nosy technician could not take it out.

I changed arms, picked up tools, and remembered to take those hundred Joe Millers in print-out. "Goodnight, Mike."

"Goodnight, Man. Thank you. Bolshoyeh thanks!"

2

I took Trans-Crisium tube to L-City but did not go home; Mike had asked about a meeting that night at 2100 in Stilyagi Hall. Mike monitored concerts, meetings, and so forth; someone had switched off by hand his pickups in Stilyagi Hall. I suppose he felt rebuffed.

I could guess why they had been switched off. Politics—turned out to be a protest meeting. What use it was to bar Mike from talk-talk I could not see, since was a cinch bet that Warden's stoolies would be in crowd. Not that any attempt to stop meeting was expected, or even to discipline undischarged transportees who chose to sound off. Wasn't necessary.

My Grandfather Stone claimed that Luna was only open prison in history. No bars, no guards, no rules—and no need for them. Back in early days, he said, before was clear that transportation was a life sentence, some lags tried to escape. By ship, of course—and, since a ship is mass-rated almost to a gram, that meant a ship's officer had to be bribed.

Some were bribed, they say. But were no escapes; man who takes bribe doesn't necessarily stay bribed. I recall seeing a man just after eliminated through East Lock; don't suppose a corpse eliminated in orbit looks prettier.

So wardens didn't fret about protest meetings. "Let 'em yap" was policy. Yapping had same significance as squeals of kittens in a box. Oh, some wardens listened and other wardens tried to suppress it but added up same either way—null program.

When Mort the Wart took office in 2068, he gave us a sermon about how things were going to be different "on" Luna in his administration—noise about "a mundane paradise wrought with our own strong hands" and "putting our shoulders to the wheel together, in a spirit of brotherhood" and "let past mistakes be forgotten as we turn our faces toward the bright, new dawn." I heard it in Mother Boor's Tucker Bag while inhaling Irish stew and a liter of her Aussie brew. I remember her comment: "He talks purty, don't he?"

Her comment was only result. Some petitions were submitted and Warden's bodyguards started carrying new type of gun; no other changes. After he had been here a while he quit making appearances even by video.

So I went to meeting merely because Mike was curious. When I checked my p-suit and kit at West Lock tube station, I took a test recorder and placed in my belt pouch, so that Mike would have a full account even if I fell asleep.

But almost didn't go in. I came up from level 7-A and started in through a side door and was stopped by a stilyagi—padded tights, codpiece and calves, torso shined and sprinkled with stardust. Not that I care how people dress; I was wearing tights myself (unpadded) and sometimes oil my upper body on social occasions.

But I don't use cosmetics and my hair was too thin to ruck up in a scalp lock. This boy had scalp shaved on sides and his lock built up to fit a rooster and had topped it with a red cap with bulge in front.

A Liberty Cap—first I ever saw. I started to crowd past; he shoved arm across and pushed face at mine. "Your ticket!"

"Sorry," I said. "Didn't know. Where do I buy it?"

"You don't."

"Repeat," I said. "You faded."

"Nobody," he growled, "gets in without being vouched for. Who are you?"

"I am," I answered carefully, "Manuel Garcia O'Kelly, and old cobbers all know me. Who are *you?*"

"Never mind! Show a ticket with right chop, or out y' go!"

I wondered about his life expectancy. Tourists often remark on how polite everybody is in Luna—with unstated comment that ex-prison shouldn't be so civilized. Having been Earthside and seen what *they* put up with, I know what they mean. But useless to tell them we are what we are because bad actors don't live long—in Luna.

But had no intention of fighting no matter how new-chum this lad behaved; I simply thought about how his face would look if I brushed number-seven arm across his mouth.

Just a thought—I was about to answer politely when I saw Shorty Mkrum inside. Shorty was a big black fellow two meters tall, sent up to The Rock for murder, and sweetest, most helpful man I've ever worked with—taught him laser drilling before I burned my arm off. "Shorty!"

He heard me and grinned like an eighty-eight. "Hi, Mannie!" He moved toward us. "Glad you came, Man!"

17

"Not sure I have," I said. "Blockage on line."

"Doesn't have a ticket," said doorman.

Shorty reached into his pouch, put one in my hand. "Now he does. Come on, Mannie."

"Show me chop on it," insisted doorman.

"It's my chop," Shorty said softly. "Okay, tovarishch?"

Nobody argued with Shorty—don't see how he got involved in murder. We moved down front where vip row was reserved. "Want you to meet a nice little girl," said Shorty.

She was "little" only to Shorty. I'm not short, 175 cm., but she was taller—180, I learned later, and massed 70 kilos, all curves and as blond as Shorty was black. I decided she must be transportee since colors rarely stay that clear past first generation. Pleasant face, quite pretty, and mop of yellow curls topped off that long, blond, solid, lovely structure.

I stopped three paces away to look her up and down and whistle. She held her pose, then nodded to thank me but abruptly—bored with compliments, no doubt. Shorty waited till formality was over, then said softly, "Wyoh, this is Comrade Mannie, best drillman that ever drifted a tunnel. Mannie, this little girl is Wyoming Knott and she came all the way from Plato to tell us how we're doing in Hong Kong. Wasn't that sweet of her?"

She touched hands with me. "Call me Wye, Mannie—but don't say 'Why not.' "

I almost did but controlled it and said, "Okay, Wye." She went on, glancing at my bare head, "So you're a miner. Shorty, where's his cap? I thought the miners over here were organized." She and Shorty were wearing little red hats like doorman's—as were maybe a third of crowd.

"No longer a miner," I explained. "That was before I lost this wing." Raised left arm, let her see seam joining prosthetic to meat arm (I never mind calling it to a woman's attention; puts some off but arouses maternal in others—averages). "These days I'm a computerman."

She said sharply, "You fink for the Authority?"

Even today, with almost as many women in Luna as men, I'm too much old-timer to be rude to a woman no matter what—they have so much of what we have none of. But she had flicked scar tissue and I answered almost sharply, "I am *not* employee of Warden. I do business with Authority—as private contractor."

"That's okay," she answered, her voice warm again. "Everybody does business with the Authority, we can't avoid it—and that's the trouble. That's what we're going to change."

18

We are, eh? How? I thought. *Everybody does business with Authority for same reason everybody does business with Law of Gravitation. Going to change that, too?* But kept thoughts to myself, not wishing to argue with a lady.

"Mannie's okay," Shorty said gently. "He's mean as they come—I vouch for him. Here's a cap for him," he added, reaching into pouch. He started to set it on my head.

Wyoming Knott took it from him. "You sponsor him?"

"I said so."

"Okay, here's how we do it in Hong Kong." Wyoming stood in front of me, placed cap on my head—kissed me firmly on mouth.

She didn't hurry. Being kissed by Wyoming Knott is more definite than being married to most women. Had I been Mike all my lights would have flashed at once. I felt like a Cyborg with pleasure center switched on.

Presently I realized it was over and people were whistling. I blinked and said, "I'm glad I joined. What have I joined?"

Wyoming said, "Don't you know?" Shorty cut in, "Meeting's about to start—he'll find out. Sit down, Man. Please sit down, Wyoh." So we did as a man was banging a gavel.

With gavel and an amplifier at high gain he made himself heard. "Shut doors!" he shouted. "This is a closed meeting. Check man in front of you, behind you, each side—if you don't know him and nobody you know can vouch for him, throw him out!"

"Throw him out, hell!" somebody answered. "Eliminate him out nearest lock!"

"Quiet, please! Someday we will." There was milling around, and a scuffle in which one man's red cap was snatched from head and he was thrown out, sailing beautifully and still rising as he passed through door. Doubt if he felt it; think he was unconscious. A woman was ejected politely—not politely on her part; she made coarse remarks about ejectors. I was embarrassed.

At last doors were closed. Music started, banner unfolded over platform. It read: LIBERTY! EQUALITY! FRATERNITY! Everybody whistled; some started to sing, loudly and badly: "Arise, Ye Prisoners of Starvation—" Can't say anybody looked starved. But reminded me I hadn't eaten since 1400; hoped it would not last long—and that reminded me that my recorder was good for only two hours—and that made me wonder what would happen if they knew? Sail me through air to land with sickening grunch? Or eliminate me? But didn't worry; made that recorder myself, using number-three arm,

19

and nobody but a miniaturization mechanic would figure out what it was.

Then came speeches.

Semantic content was low to negative. One bloke proposed that we march on Warden's Residence, "shoulder to shoulder," and demand our rights. Picture it. Do we do this in tube capsules, then climb out one at a time at his private station? What are his bodyguards doing? Or do we put on p-suits and stroll across surface to his upper lock? With laser drills and plenty of power you can open any airlock—but how about farther down? Is lift running? Jury-rig hoist and go down anyhow, then tackle next lock?

I don't care for such work at zero pressure; mishap in pressure suit is too permanent—especially when somebody arranges mishap. One first thing learned about Luna, back with first shiploads of convicts, was that zero pressure was place for good manners. Bad-tempered straw boss didn't last many shifts; had an "accident"—and top bosses learned not to pry into accidents or they met accidents, too. Attrition ran 70 percent in early years—but those who lived were nice people. Not tame, not soft, Luna is not for them. But well-behaved.

But seemed to me that every hothead in Luna was in Stilyagi Hall that night. They whistled and cheered this shoulder-to-shoulder noise.

After discussion opened, some sense was talked. One shy little fellow with bloodshot eyes of old-time drillman stood up. "I'm an ice miner," he said. "Learned my trade doing time for Warden like most of you. I've been on my own thirty years and done okay. Raised eight kids and all of 'em earned way—none eliminated nor any serious trouble. I should say I *did* do okay . . . because today you have to listen farther out or deeper down to find ice.

"That's okay, still ice in The Rock and a miner expects to sound for it. But Authority pays same price for ice now as thirty years ago. And that's not okay. Worse yet, Authority scrip doesn't buy what it used to. I remember when Hong Kong Luna dollars swapped even for Authority dollars— Now it takes three Authority dollars to match one HKL dollar. *I* don't know what to do . . . but I know it takes ice to keep warrens and farms going."

He sat down, looking sad. Nobody whistled but everybody wanted to talk. Next character pointed out that water can be extracted from rock—this is news? Some rock runs 6 percent—but such rock is scarcer than fossil water. Why can't people do arithmetic?

Several farmers bellyached and one wheat farmer was typical. "You heard what Fred Hauser said about ice. Fred, Authority isn't passing along that low price to farmers. I started almost as long ago as you did, with one two-kilometer tunnel leased from Authority. My oldest son and I sealed and pressured it and we had a pocket of ice and made our first crop simply on a bank loan to cover power and lighting fixtures, seed and chemicals.

"We kept extending tunnels and buying lights and planting better seed and now we get nine times as much per hectare as the best open-air farming down Earthside. What does that make us? Rich? Fred, we owe more *now* than we did the day we went private! If I sold out—if anybody was fool enough to buy—I'd be bankrupt. Why? Because I *have* to buy water from Authority—and have to sell my wheat to Authority—and never close gap. Twenty years ago I bought city sewage from the Authority, sterilized and processed it myself and made a profit on a crop. But *today* when I buy sewage, I'm charged distilled-water price and on top of that for the solids. Yet price of a tonne of wheat at catapult head is just what it was twenty years ago. Fred, you said you didn't know what to do. *I* can tell you! Get *rid* of Authority!"

They whistled for him. *A fine idea*, I thought, *but who bells cat?*

Wyoming Knott, apparently—chairman stepped back and let Shorty introduce her as a "brave little girl who's come all the way from Hong Kong Luna to tell how our Chinee comrades cope with situation"—and choice of words showed that he had never been there . . . not surprising; in 2075, HKL tube ended at Endsville, leaving a thousand kilometers of maria to do by rolligon bus, Serenitatis and part of Tranquillitatis—expensive and dangerous. I'd been there—but on contract, via mail rocket.

Before travel became cheap many people in Luna City and Novylen thought that Hong Kong Luna was all Chinee. But Hong Kong was as mixed as we were. Great China dumped what she didn't want there, first from Old Hong Kong and Singapore, then Aussies and Enzees and black fellows and marys and Malays and Tamil and name it. Even Old Bolshies from Vladivostok and Harbin and Ulan Bator. Wye looked Svenska and had British last name with North American first name but could have been Russki. My word, a Loonie then rarely knew who father was and, if raised in crêche, might be vague about mother.

21

I thought Wyoming was going to be too shy to speak. She stood there, looking scared and *little,* with Shorty towering over her, a big, black mountain. She waited until admiring whistles died down. Luna City was two-to-one male then, that meeting ran about ten-to-one; she could have recited ABC and they would have applauded.

Then she tore into them.

"You! You're a wheat farmer—going broke. Do you know how much a Hindu housewife pays for a kilo of flour made from your wheat? How much a tonne of your wheat fetches in Bombay? How little it costs the Authority to get it from catapult head to Indian Ocean? Downhill all the way! Just solid-fuel retros to brake it—and where do those come from? Right here! And what do *you* get in return? A few shiploads of fancy goods, owned by the Authority and priced high because it's importado. Importado, importado!—I never *touch* importado! If we don't make it in Hong Kong, I don't use it. What else do you get for wheat? The privilege of selling Lunar ice to Lunar Authority, buying it back as washing water, then *giving* it to the Authority—then buying it back a second time as flushing water—then *giving it again* to the Authority with valuable solids added—then buying it a *third* time at still higher price for farming—then you sell that wheat to the Authority at *their* price—and buy power from the Authority to grow it, again at *their* price! *Lunar* power—not one kilowatt up from Terra. It comes from Lunar ice and Lunar steel, or sunshine spilled on Luna's soil—all put together by *loonies!* Oh, you rockheads, you *deserve* to starve!"

She got silence more respectful than whistles. At last a peevish voice said, "What do you expect us to do, gospazha? Throw rocks at Warden?"

Wyoh smiled. "Yes, we could throw rocks. But the solution is so simple that you all know it. Here in Luna we're rich. Three million hardworking, smart, skilled people, enough water, plenty of everything, endless power, endless cubic. *But* . . . what we *don't* have is a free market. *We must get rid of the Authority!"*

"Yes—but how?"

"Solidarity. In HKL we're learning. Authority charges too much for water, don't buy. It pays too little for ice, don't sell. It holds monopoly on export, don't export. Down in Bombay they want wheat. If it doesn't arrive, the day will come when brokers come here to bid for it—at triple or more the present prices!"

"What do we do in meantime? Starve?"

Same peevish voice— Wyoming picked him out, let her head roll in that old gesture by which a Loonie fem says, *"You're too fat for me!"* She said, "In your case, cobber, it wouldn't hurt."

Guffaws shut him up. Wyoh went on, "No one need starve. Fred Hauser, fetch your drill to Hong Kong; the Authority doesn't own our water and air system and we pay what ice is worth. You with the bankrupt farm—if you have the guts to admit that you're bankrupt, come to Hong Kong and start over. We have a chronic labor shortage, a hard worker doesn't starve." She looked around and added, "I've said enough. It's up to you"—left platform, sat down between Shorty and myself.

She was trembling. Shorty patted her hand; she threw him a glance of thanks, then whispered to me, "How did I do?"

"Wonderful," I assured her. "Terrific!" She seemed reassured.

But I hadn't been honest. "Wonderful" she had been, at swaying crowd. But oratory is a null program. That we were slaves I had known all my life—and nothing could be done about it. True, we weren't bought and sold—but as long as Authority held monopoly over what we had to have and what we could sell to buy it, we were slaves.

But what could we do? Warden wasn't our owner. Had he been, some way could be found to eliminate him. But Lunar Authority was not in Luna, it was on Terra—and we had not one ship, not even small hydrogen bomb. There weren't even hand guns in Luna, though what we would do with guns I did not know. Shoot each other, maybe.

Three million, unarmed and helpless—and eleven *billion* of them . . . with ships and bombs and weapons. We could be a nuisance—but how long will papa take it before baby gets spanked?

I wasn't impressed. As it says in Bible, God fights on side of heaviest artillery.

They cackled again, what to do, how to organize, and so forth, and again we heard that "shoulder to shoulder" noise. Chairman had to use gavel and I began to fidget.

But sat up when I heard familiar voice: "Mr. Chairman! May I have the indulgence of the house for five minutes?"

I looked around. Professor Bernardo de la Paz—which could have guessed from old-fashioned way of talking even if hadn't known voice. Distinguished man with wavy white hair, dimples in cheeks, and voice that smiled— Don't know how old he was but was old when I first met him, as a boy.

He had been transported before I was born but was not a lag. He was a political exile like Warden, but a subversive and instead of fat job like "warden," Professor had been dumped, to live or starve.

No doubt he could have gone to work in any school then in L-City but he didn't. He worked a while washing dishes, I've heard, then as babysitter, expanding into a nursery school, and then into a crêche. When I met him he was running a crêche, and a boarding and day school, from nursery through primary, middle, and high schools, employed co-op thirty teachers, and was adding college courses.

Never boarded with him but I studied under him. I was opted at fourteen and my new family sent me to school, as I had had only three years, plus spotty tutoring. My eldest wife was a firm woman and made me go to school.

I liked Prof. He would teach *anything*. Wouldn't matter that he knew nothing about it; if pupil wanted it, he would smile and set a price, locate materials, stay a few lessons ahead. Or barely even if he found it tough—never pretended to know more than he did. Took algebra from him and by time we reached cubics I corrected his probs as often as he did mine—but he charged into each lesson gaily.

I started electronics under him, soon was teaching him. So he stopped charging and we went along together until he dug up an engineer willing to daylight for extra money —whereupon we both paid new teacher and Prof tried to stick with me, thumb-fingered and slow, but happy to be stretching his mind.

Chairman banged gavel. "We are glad to extend to Professor de la Paz as much time as he wants—and you chooms in back sign off! Before I use this mallet on skulls."

Prof came forward and they were as near silent as Loonies ever are; he was respected. "I shan't be long," he started in. Stopped to look at Wyoming, giving her up-and-down and whistling. "Lovely señorita," he said, "can this poor one be forgiven? I have the painful duty of disagreeing with your eloquent manifesto."

Wyoh bristled. "Disagree how? What I said was true!"

"Please! Only on one point. May I proceed?"

"Uh . . . go ahead."

"You are right that the Authority must go. It is ridiculous—pestilential, not to be borne—that we should be ruled by an irresponsible dictator in all our essential economy! It strikes at the most basic human right, the right to bargain in a free marketplace. But I respectfully suggest that you erred in saying that we should sell wheat to Terra—or rice, or any food—at *any* price. We must *not* export food!"

That wheat farmer broke in. "What am I going to do with all that wheat?"

"Please! It would be right to ship wheat to Terra . . . if tonne for tonne they returned it. As water. As nitrates. As phosphates. Tonne for tonne. Otherwise no price is high enough."

Wyoming said "Just a moment" to farmer, then to Prof: "They can't and you know it. It's cheap to ship downhill, expensive to ship uphill. But we don't need water and plant chemicals, what *we* need is not so massy. Instruments. Drugs. Processes. Some machinery. Control tapes. I've given this much study, sir. If we can get fair prices in a free market—"

"Please, miss! May I continue?"

"Go ahead. I want to rebut."

"Fred Hauser told us that ice is harder to find. Too true —bad news now and disastrous for our grandchildren. Luna City should use the same water today we used twenty years ago . . . plus enough ice mining for population increase. But we use water *once*—one full cycle, three different ways. Then we ship it to India. As wheat. Even though wheat is vacuum-processed, it contains precious water. Why ship water to India? They have the whole Indian Ocean! And the remaining mass of that grain is even more disastrously expensive, plant foods still harder to come by, even though we extract them from rock. Comrades, harken to me! Every load you ship to Terra condemns your grandchildren to slow death. The miracle of photosynthesis, the plant-and-animal cycle, is a *closed* cycle. You have opened it—and your lifeblood runs downhill to Terra. You don't need higher prices, one cannot eat money! What you need, what we all need, is an end to this loss. Embargo, utter and absolute. *Luna must be self-sufficient!*"

A dozen people shouted to be heard and more were talking, while chairman banged gavel. So I missed interruption until woman screamed, then I looked around.

All doors were now open and I saw three armed men in one nearest—men in yellow uniform of Warden's bodyguard. At main door in back one was using a bull voice; drowned out crowd noise and sound system. "ALL RIGHT, ALL RIGHT!" it boomed. "STAY WHERE YOU ARE. YOU ARE UNDER ARREST. DON'T MOVE, KEEP QUIET. FILE OUT ONE AT A TIME, HANDS EMPTY AND STRETCHED OUT IN FRONT OF YOU."

Shorty picked up man next to him and threw him at guards nearest; two went down, third fired. Somebody shrieked. Skinny little girl, redhead, eleven or twelve, launched self at third guard's knees and hit rolled up in ball; down he went. Shorty swung hand behind him, pushing Wyoming Knott into shelter of his big frame, shouted over shoulder, "Take care of Wyoh, Man—stick close!" as he moved toward door, parting crowd right and left like children.

More screams and I whiffed something—stink I had smelled day I lost arm and knew with horror were not stun guns but laser beams. Shorty reached door and grabbed a guard with each big hand. Little redhead was out of sight; guard she had bowled over was on hands and knees. I swung left arm at his face and felt jar in shoulder as his jaw broke. Must have hesitated for Shorty pushed me and yelled, "Move, Man! Get her out of here!"

I grabbed Wyoming's waist with right arm, swung her over guard I had quieted and through door—with trouble; she didn't seem to want to be rescued. She slowed again beyond door; I shoved her hard in buttocks, forcing her to run rather than fall. I glanced back.

Shorty had other two guards each by neck; he grinned as he cracked skulls together. They popped like eggs and he yelled at me: *"Git!"*

I left, chasing Wyoming. Shorty needed no help, nor ever would again—nor could I waste his last effort. For I did see that, while killing those guards, he was standing on one leg. Other was gone at hip.

3

Wyoh was halfway up ramp to level six before I caught up. She didn't slow and I had to grab door handle to get into pressure lock with her. There I stopped her, pulled red cap off her curls and stuck it in my pouch. "That's better." Mine was missing.

She looked startled. But answered, "Da. It is."

"Before we open door," I said, "are you running anywhere particular? And do I stay and hold them off? Or go with?"

"I don't know. We'd better wait for Shorty."

"Shorty's dead."

Eyes widened, she said nothing. I went on, "Were you staying with him? Or somebody?"

"I was booked for a hotel—Gostaneetsa Ukraina. I don't know where it is. I got here too late to buy in."

"Mmm— That's one place you won't go. Wyoming, I don't know what's going on. First time·in months I've seen any Warden's bodyguard in L-City . . . and *never* seen one not escorting vip. Uh, could take you home with me—but they may be looking for me, too. Anywise, ought to get out of public corridors."

Came pounding on door from level-six side and a little face peered up through glass bull's-eye. "Can't stay here," I added, opening door. Was a little girl no higher than my waist. She looked up scornfully and said, "Kiss her somewhere else. You're blocking traffic." Squeezed between us as I opened second door for her.

"Let's take her advice," I said, "and suggest you take my arm and try to look like I was man you want to be with. We stroll. Slow."

So we did. Was side corridor with little traffic other than children always underfoot. If Wart's bodyguards tried to track us, Earthside cop style, a dozen or ninety kids could tell which way tall blonde went—if any Loonie child would give stooge of Warden so much as time of day.

A boy almost old enough to appreciate Wyoming stopped in front of us and gave her a happy whistle. She smiled and waved him aside. "There's our trouble," I said in her ear. "You stand out like Terra at full. Ought to duck into a hotel. One off next side corridor—nothing much, bundling booths mostly. But close."

"I'm in no mood to bundle."

"Wyoh, please! Wasn't asking. Could take separate rooms."

"Sorry. Could you find me a W.C.? And is there a chemist's shop near?"

"Trouble?"

"Not that sort. A W.C. to get me out of sight—for I *am* conspicuous—and a chemist's shop for cosmetics. Body makeup. And for my hair, too."

First was easy, one at hand. When she was locked in, I found a chemist's shop, asked how much body makeup to cover a girl so tall—marked a point under my chin—and massing

27

forty-eight? I bought that amount in sepia, went to another shop and bought same amount—winning roll at first shop, losing at second—came out even. Then I bought black hair tint at third shop—and a red dress.

Wyoming was wearing black shorts and pullover—practical for travel and effective on a blonde. But I'd been married all my life and had some notion of what women wear and had *never* seen a woman with dark sepia skin, shade of makeup, wear black by choice. Furthermore, skirts were worn in Luna City then by dressy women. This shift was a skirt with bib and price convinced me it must be dressy. Had to guess at size but material had some stretch.

Ran into three people who knew me but was no unusual comment. Nobody seemed excited, trade going on as usual; hard to believe that a riot had taken place minutes ago on level below and a few hundred meters north. I set it aside for later thought—excitement was not what I wanted.

I took stuff to Wye, buzzing door and passing in it; then stashed self in a taproom for half an hour and half a liter and watched video. Still no excitement, no "we interrupt for special bulletin." I went back, buzzed, and waited.

Wyoming came out—and I didn't recognize her. Then did and stopped to give full applause. Just had to—whistles and finger snaps and moans and a scan like mapping radar.

Wyoh was now darker than I am, and pigment had gone on beautifully. Must have been carrying items in pouch as eyes were dark now, with lashes to match, and mouth was dark red and bigger. She had used black hair tint, then frizzed hair up with grease as if to take kinks out, and her tight curls had defeated it enough to make convincingly imperfect. She didn't look Afro—but not European, either. Seemed some mixed breed, and thereby more a Loonie.

Red dress was too small. Clung like sprayed enamel and flared out at mid-thigh with permanent static charge. She had taken shoulder strap off her pouch and had it under arm. Shoes she had discarded or pouched; bare feet made her shorter.

She looked good. Better yet, she looked not at all like agitatrix who had harangued crowd.

She waited, big smile on face and body undulating, while I applauded. Before I was done, two little boys flanked me and added shrill endorsements, along with clog steps. So I tipped them and told them to be missing; Wyoming flowed to me and took my arm. "Is it okay? Will I pass?"

"Wyoh, you look like slot-machine sheila waiting for action."

28

"Why, you drecklich choom! Do I look like slot-machine prices? Tourist!"

"Don't jump salty, beautiful. Name a gift. Then speak my name. If it's bread-and-honey, I own a hive."

"Uh—" She fisted me solidly in ribs, grinned. "I was flying, cobber. If I ever bundle with you—not likely—we won't speak to the bee. Let's find that hotel."

So we did and I bought a key. Wyoming put on a show but needn't have bothered. Night clerk never looked up from his knitting, didn't offer to roll. Once inside, Wyoming threw bolts. "It's nice!"

Should have been, at thirty-two Hong Kong dollars. I think she expected a booth but I would not put her in such, even to hide. Was comfortable lounge with own bath and no water limit. And phone and delivery lift, which I needed.

She started to open pouch. "I saw what you paid. Let's settle it, so that—"

I reached over, closed her pouch. "Was to be no mention of bees."

"What? Oh, merde, that was about bundling. You got this doss for me and it's only right that—"

"Switch off."

"Uh . . . half? No grievin' with Steven."

"Nyet. Wyoh, you're a long way from home. What money you have, hang on to."

"Manuel O'Kelly, if you don't let me pay my share, I'll walk out of here!"

I bowed. "Dosvedanyuh, Gospazha, ee sp'coynoynochi. I hope we shall meet again." I moved to unbolt door.

She glared, then closed pouch savagely. "I'll stay. M'goy!"

"You're welcome."

"I mean it, I really do thank you, Just the same— Well, I'm not used to accepting favors. I'm a Free Woman."

"Congratulations. I think."

"Don't you be salty, either. You're a firm man and I respect that—I'm glad you're on our side."

"Not sure I am."

"What?"

"Cool it. Am not on Warden's side. Nor will I talk . . . wouldn't want Shorty, Bog rest his generous soul, to haunt me. But your program isn't practical."

"But, Mannie, you don't understand! If all of us—"

"Hold it, Wye; this no time for politics. I'm tired and hungry. When did you eat last?"

"Oh, goodness!" Suddenly she looked small, young, tired. "I

29

don't know. On the bus, I guess. Helmet rations."

"What would you say to a Kansas City cut, rare, with baked potato, Tycho sauce, green salad, coffee . . . and a drink first?"

"Heavenly!"

"I think so too, but we'll be lucky, this hour in this hole, to get algae soup and burgers. What do you drink?"

"Anything. Ethanol."

"Okay." I went to lift, punched for service. "Menu, please." It displayed and I settled for prime rib plus rest, and two orders of apfelstrudel with whipped cream. I added a half liter of table vodka and ice and starred that part.

"Is there time for me to take a bath? Would you mind?"

"Go ahead, Wye. You'll smell better."

"Louse. Twelve hours in a p-suit and you'd stink, too—the bus was dreadful. I'll hurry."

"Half a sec, Wye. Does that stuff wash off? You may need it when you leave . . . whenever you do, wherever you go."

"Yes, it does. But you bought three times as much as I used. I'm sorry, Mannie; I plan to carry makeup on political trips—things can happen. Like tonight, though tonight was worst. But I ran short of seconds and missed a capsule and almost missed the bus."

"So go scrub."

"Yes, sir, Captain. Uh, I *don't* need help to scrub my back . . . but I'll leave the door up so we can talk. Just for company, no invitation implied."

"Suit yourself. I've seen a woman."

"What a thrill that must have been for her." She grinned and fisted me another in ribs—hard—went in and started tub. "Mannie, would you like to bathe in it first? Secondhand water is good enough for this makeup and that stink you complained about."

"Unmetered water, dear. Run it deep."

"Oh, what luxury! At home I use the same bath water three days running." She whistled softly and happily. "Are you wealthy, Mannie?"

"Not wealthy, not weeping."

Lift jingled; I answered, fixed basic martinis, vodka over ice, handed hers in, got out and sat down, out of sight—nor had I seen sights; she was shoulder deep in happy suds. "Pawlnoi Zheezni!" I called.

"A full life to you, too, Mannie. Just the medicine I needed." After pause for medicine she went on, "Mannie, you're married. Ja?"

"Da. It shows?"

"Quite. You're nice to a woman but not eager and quite independent. So you're married and long married. Children?"

"Seventeen divided by four."

"Clan marriage?"

"Line. Opted at fourteen and I'm fifth of nine. So seventeen kids is nominal. Big family."

"It must be nice. I've never seen much of line families, not many in Hong Kong. Plenty of clans and groups and lots of polyandries but the line way never took hold."

"*Is* nice. Our marriage nearly a hundred years old. Dates back to Johnson City and first transportees—twenty-one links, nine alive today, never a divorce. Oh, it's a madhouse when our descendants and inlaws and kinfolk get together for birthday or wedding—more kids than seventeen, of course; we don't count 'em after they marry or I'd have 'children' old enough to be my grandfather. Happy way to live, never much pressure. Take me. Nobody woofs if I stay away a week and don't phone. Welcome when I show up. Line marriages rarely have divorces. How could I do better?"

"I don't think you could. Is it an alternation? And what's the spacing?"

"Spacing has no rule, just what suits us. Been alternation up to latest link, last year. We married a girl when alternation called for boy. But was special."

"Special how?"

"My youngest wife is a granddaughter of eldest husband and wife. At least she's granddaughter of Mum—senior is 'Mum' or sometimes Mimi to her husbands—and she may be of Grandpaw—but not related to other spouses. So no reason not to marry back in, not even consanguinity okay in other types of marriage. None, nit, zero. And Ludmilla grew up in our family because her mother had her solo, then moved to Novylen and left her with us.

"Milla didn't want to talk about marrying out when old enough for us to think about it. She cried and asked us *please* to make an exception. So we did. Grandpaw doesn't figure in genetic angle—these days his interest in women is more gallant than practical. As senior husband he spent our wedding night with her—but consummation was only formal. Number-two husband, Greg, took care of it later and everybody pretended. And everybody happy. Ludmilla is a sweet little thing, just fifteen and pregnant first time."

"Your baby?"

"Greg's, I think. Oh, mine too, but in fact was in Novy Leningrad. Probably Greg's, unless Milla got outside help. But didn't, she's a home girl. And a wonderful cook."

Lift rang; took care of it, folded down table, opened chairs, paid bill and sent lift up. "Throw it to pigs?"

"I'm coming! Mind if I don't do my face?"

"Come in skin for all of me."

"For two dimes I would, you much-married man." She came out quickly, blond again and hair slicked back and damp. Had not put on black outfit; again in dress I bought. Red suited her. She sat down, lifted covers off food. "Oh, boy! Mannie, would your family marry me? You're a dinkum provider."

"I'll ask. Must be unanimous."

"Don't crowd yourself." She picked up sticks, got busy. About a thousand calories later she said, "I told you I was a Free Woman. I wasn't, always."

I waited. Women talk when they want to. Or don't.

"When I was fifteen I married two brothers, twins twice my age and I was terribly happy."

She fiddled with what was on plate, then seemed to change subject. "Mannie, that was just static about wanting to marry your family. You're safe from me. If I ever marry again—unlikely but I'm not opposed to it—it would be just one man, a tight little marriage, earthworm style. Oh, I don't mean I would keep him dogged down. I don't think it matters where a man eats lunch as long as he comes home for dinner. I would try to make him happy."

"Twins didn't get along?"

"Oh, not that at all. I got pregnant and we were all delighted . . . and I had it, and it was a monster and had to be eliminated. They were good to me about it. But I can read print. I announced a divorce, had myself sterilized, moved from Novylen to Hong Kong, and started over as a Free Woman."

"Wasn't that drastic? Male parent oftener than female; men are exposed more."

"Not in my case. We had it calculated by the best mathematical geneticist in Novy Leningrad—one of the best in Sovunion before she got shipped. I know what happened to me. I was a volunteeer colonist—I mean my mother was for I was only five. My father was transported and Mother chose to go with him and take me along. There was a solar storm warning but the pilot thought he could make it—or didn't care; he was a Cyborg. He did make it but we got hit on the ground—and, Mannie, that's one thing that pushed me into politics, that ship sat four hours before they let us disembark. Authority red tape, quarantine perhaps; I was too young to know. But I wasn't too young later to figure out that I had birthed a monster because the Authority doesn't *care* what happens to us outcasts."

"Can't start argument; they *don't* care. But, Wyoh, still sounds hasty. If you caught damage from radiation—well, no geneticist but know something about radiation. So you had a damaged egg. Does *not* mean egg next to it was hurt—statistically unlikely."

"Oh, I know that."

"Mmmm— What sterilization? Radical? Or contraceptive?"

"Contraceptive. My tubes could be opened. But, Mannie, a woman who has had one monster doesn't risk it again." She touched my prosthetic. "You have that. Doesn't it make you eight times as careful not to risk this one?" She touched my meat arm. "That's the way I feel. You have *that* to contend with; I have *this*—and I would never told you if you hadn't been hurt, too."

I didn't say left arm more versatile than right—she was correct; don't want to trade in right arm. Need it to pat girls if naught else. "Still think you could have healthy babies."

"O, I can! I've had eight."

"Huh?"

"I'm a professional host-mother, Mannie."

I opened mouth, closed it. Idea wasn't strange. I read Earthside papers. But doubt if any surgeon in Luna City in 2075 ever performed such transplant. In cows, yes—but L-City females unlikely at any price to have babies for other women; even homely ones could get husband or six. (Correction: Are *no* homely women. Some more beautiful than others.)

Glanced at her figure, quickly looked up. She said, "Don't strain your eyes, Mannie; I'm not carrying now. Too busy with politics. But hosting is a good profession for Free Woman. It's high pay. Some Chinee families are wealthy and all my babies have been Chinee—and Chinee are smaller than average and I'm a big cow; a two-and-a-half- or three-kilo Chinese baby is no trouble. Doesn't spoil my figure. These—" She glanced down at her lovelies. "I don't wet-nurse them, I never *see* them. So I look nulliparous and younger than I am, maybe.

"But I didn't know how well it suited me when I first heard of it. I was clerking in a Hindu shop, eating money, no more, when I saw this ad in the Hong Kong Gong. It was the thought of having a baby, a *good* baby, that hooked me; I was still in emotional trauma from my monster—and it turned out to be just what Wyoming needed. I stopped feeling that I was a failure as a woman. I made more money than I could ever

33

hope to earn at other jobs. And my time almost to myself; having a baby hardly slows me down—six weeks at most and that long only because I want to be fair to my clients; a baby is a valuable property. And I was soon in politics; I sounded off and the underground got in touch with me. That's when I started *living*, Mannie; I studied politics and economics and history and learned to speak in public and turned out to have a flair for organization. It's satisfying work because I believe in it—I *know* that Luna will be free. Only— Well, it would be nice to have a husband to come home to . . . if he didn't mind that I was sterile. But I don't think about it; I'm too busy. Hearing about your nice family got me talking, that's all. I must apologize for having bored you."

How many women apologize? But Wyoh was more man than woman some ways, despite eight Chinee babies. "Wasn't bored."

"I hope not. Mannie, why do you say our program isn't practical? We need you."

Suddenly felt tired. How to tell lovely woman dearest dream is nonsense? "Um. Wyoh, let's start over. You told them what to do. But will they? Take those two you singled out. All that iceman knows, bet anything, is how to dig ice. So he'll go on digging and selling to Authority because that's what he can do. Same for wheat farmer. Years ago, he put in one cash crop— now he's got ring in nose. If he wanted to be independent, would have diversified. Raised what he eats, sold rest free market and stayed away from catapult head. I *know*—I'm a farm boy."

"You said you were a computerman."

"Am, and that's a piece of same picture. I'm not a top computerman. But best in Luna. I won't go civil service, so Authority has to hire me when in trouble—my prices—or send Earthside, pay risk and hardship, then ship him back fast before his body forgets Terra. At far more than I charge. So if I can do it, I get their jobs—and Authority can't touch me; was born free. And if no work—usually is—I stay home and eat high.

"We've got a proper farm, not a one-cash-crop deal. Chickens. Small herd of whiteface, plus milch cows. Pigs. Mutated fruit tress. Vegetables. A little wheat and grind it ourselves and don't insist on white flour, and sell—free market— what's left. Make own beer and brandy. I learned drillman extending our tunnels. Everybody works, not too hard. Kids make cattle take exercise by switching them along; don't use tread mill. Kids gather eggs and feed chickens, don't use much machinery. Air we can buy from L-City—aren't far out of town and pressure-tunnel connected. But more often we sell air; being farm, cycle shows Oh-two excess. Always have valuta to meet bills."

"How about water and power?"

"Not expensive. We collect some power, sunshine screens on surface, and have a little pocket of ice. Wye, our farm was founded before year two thousand, when L-City was one natural cave, and we've kept improving it—advantage of line marriage; doesn't die and capital improvements add up."

"But surely your ice won't last forever?"

"Well, now—" I scratched head and grinned. "We're careful; we keep our sewage and garbage and sterilize and use it. Never put a drop back into city system. But—don't tell Warden, dear, but back when Greg was teaching me to drill, we happened to drill into bottom of main south reservoir—and had a tap with us, spilled hardly a drop. But we *do* buy some metered water, looks better—and ice pocket accounts for not buying much. As for power—well, power is even easier to steal. I'm a good electrician, Wyoh."

"Oh, *wonderful!*" Wyoming paid me a long whistle and looked delighted. "Everybody should do that!"

"Hope not, would show. Let 'em think up own ways to outwit Authority; our family always has. But back to your plan, Wyoh: two things wrong. Never get 'solidarity'; blokes like Hauser would cave in—because they *are* in a trap; can't hold out. Second place, suppose you managed it. Solidarity. So solid not a tonne of grain is delivered to catapult head. Forget ice; it's grain that makes Authority important and not just neutral agency it was set up to be. No grain. What happens?"

"Why, they have to negotiate a fair price, that's what!"

"My dear, you and your comrades listen to each other too much. Authority would call it rebellion and warship would orbit with bombs earmarked for L-City and Hong Kong and Tycho Under and Churchill and Novylen, troops would land, grain barges would lift, under guard—and farmers would break necks to cooperate. Terra has guns and power and bombs and ships and won't hold still for trouble from ex-cons. And troublemakers like you—and me; with you in spirit—us lousy troublemakers will be rounded up and eliminated, teach us a lesson. And earthworms would say we had it coming . . . because *our* side would never be heard. Not on Terra."

Wyoh looked stubborn. "Revolutions have succeeded before. Lenin had only a handful with him."

"Lenin moved in on a power vacuum. Wye, correct me if

35

wrong. Revolutions succeeded when—only when—governments had gone rotten soft, or disappeared."

"Not true! The American Revolution."

"South lost, nyet?"

"Not that one, the one a century earlier. They had the sort of troubles with England that we are having now—and they *won!*"

"Oh, that one. But wasn't England in trouble? France, and Spain, and Sweden—or maybe Holland? And Ireland. Ireland was rebelling; O'Kellys were in it. Wyoh, if you can stir trouble on Terra—say a war between Great China and North American Directorate, maybe PanAfrica lobbing bombs at Europe, I'd say was wizard time to kill Warden and tell Authority it's through. Not today."

"You're a pessimist."

"Nyet, realist. Never pessimist. Too much Loonie not to bet if any chance. Show me chances no worse then ten to one against and I'll go for broke. But want that one chance in ten." I pushed back chair. "Through eating?"

"Yes. Bolshoyeh spasebaw, tovarishch. It was grand!"

"My pleasure. Move to couch and I'll rid of table and dishes, —no, can't help; I'm host." I cleared table, sent up dishes, saving coffee and vodka, folded table, racked chairs, turned to speak.

She was sprawled on couch, asleep, mouth open and face softened into little girl.

Went quietly into bath and closed door. After a scrubbing I felt better—washed tights first and were dry and fit to put on by time I quit lazing in tub—don't care when world ends long as I'm bathed and in clean clothes.

Wyoh was still asleep, which made problem. Had taken room with two beds so she would not feel I was trying to talk her into bundling—not that I was against it but she had made clear she was opposed. But my bed had to be made from couch and proper bed was folded away. Should I rig it out softly, pick her up like limp baby and move her? Went back into bath and put on arm.

Then decided to wait. Phone had hush hood, Wyoh seemed unlikely to wake, and things were gnawing me. I sat down at phone, lowered hood, punched "MYCROFTXXX."

"Hi, Mike."

"Hello, Man. Have you surveyed those jokes?"

"What? Mike, haven't had a minute—and a minute may be a long time to you but it's short to me. I'll get at it as fast as I can."

36

"Okay, Man. Have you found a not-stupid for me to talk with?"

"Haven't had time for that, either. Uh . . . wait." I looked out through hood at Wyoming. "Not-stupid" in this case meant empathy . . . Wyoh had plenty. Enough to be friendly with a machine? I thought so. And could be trusted; not only had we shared trouble but she was a subversive.

"Mike, would you like to talk with a girl?"

"Girls are not-stupid?"

"Some girls are very not-stupid, Mike."

"I would like to talk with a not-stupid girl, Man."

"I'll try to arrange. But now I'm in trouble and need your help."

"I will help, Man."

"Thanks, Mike. I want to call my home—but not ordinary way. You know sometimes calls are monitored, and if Warden orders it, lock can be put on so that circuit can be traced."

"Man, you wish me to monitor your call to your home and put a lock-and-trace on it? I must inform you that I already know your home call number and the number from which you are calling."

"No, no! *Don't* want it monitored, *don't* want it locked and traced. Can *you* call my home, connect me, and control circuit so that it *can't* be monitored, *can't* be locked, *can't* be traced—even if somebody has programmed just that? Can you do it so that they won't even know their program is bypassed?"

Mike hesitated. I suppose it was a question never asked and he had to trace a few thousand possibilities to see if his control of system permitted this novel program. "Man, I can do that. I will."

"Good! Uh, program signal. If I want this sort of connection in future, I'll ask for 'Sherlock.' "

"Noted. Sherlock was my brother." Year before, I had explained to Mike how he got his name. Thereafter he read all Sherlock Holmes stories, scanning film in Luna City Carnegie Library. Don't know how he rationalized relationship; I hesitated to ask.

"Fine! Give me a 'Sherlock' to my home."

A moment later I said, "Mum? This is your favorite husband."

She answered, "Manuel! Are you in trouble again?"

I love Mum more than any other woman including my other wives, but she never stopped bringing me up—Bog willing, she never will. I tried to sound hurt. "Me? Why, you know me, Mum."

37

"I do indeed. Since you are not in trouble, perhaps you can tell me why Professor de la Paz is so anxious to get in touch with you—he has called three times—and why he wants to reach some woman with unlikely name of Wyoming Knott —and why he thinks you might be with her? Have you taken a bundling companion, Manuel, without tell me? We have freedom in our family, dear, but you know that I prefer to be told. So that I will not be taken unawares."

Mum was always jealous of all women but her co-wives and never, never, never admitted it. I said, "Mum, Bog strike me dead, I have *not* taken a bundling companion."

"Very well. You've always been a truthful boy. Now what's this mystery?"

"I'll have to ask Professor." (Not lie, just tight squeeze.) "Did he leave number?"

"No, he said he was calling from a public phone."

"Um. If he calls again, ask him to leave number and time I can reach him. This is public phone, too." (Another tight squeeze.) "In meantime— You listened to late news?"

"You know I do."

"Anything?"

"Nothing of interest."

"No excitement in L-City? Killings, riots, anything?"

"Why, no. There was a set duel in Bottom Alley but— *Manuel!* Have you killed someone?"

"No, Mum." (Breaking a man's jaw will not kill him.)

She sighed. "You'll be my death, dear. You know what I've always told you. In our family we do not brawl. Should a killing be necessary—it almost never is—matters must be discussed calmly, en famille, and proper action selected. If a new chum *must* be eliminated, other people know it. It is worth a little delay to hold good opinion and support—"

"Mum! Haven't killed anybody, don't intend to. And know that lecture by heart."

"Please be civil, dear."

"I'm sorry."

"Forgiven. Forgotten. I'm to tell Professor de la Paz to leave a number. I shall."

"One thing. Forget name 'Wyoming Knott.' Forget Professor was asking for me. If a stranger phones, or calls in person, and asks *anything* about me, you haven't heard from me, don't know where I am . . . think I've gone to Novylen. That goes for rest of family, too. Answer no questions—especially from anybody connected with Warden."

"As if I would! Manuel, you *are* in trouble."

38

"Not much and getting it fixed."—hoped!—"Tell you when I get home. Can't talk now. Love you. Switching off."

"I love you, dear. Sp'coynoynauchi."

"Thanks and you have a quiet night, too. Off."

Mum is wonderful. She was shipped up to The Rock long ago for carving a man under circumstances that left grave doubts as to girlish innocence—and has been opposed to violence and loose living ever since. Unless necessary—she's no fanatic. Bet she was a jet job as a kid and wish I'd known her—but I'm rich in sharing last half of her life.

I called Mike back. "Do you know Professor Bernardo de la Paz's voice?"

"I do, Man."

"Well . . . you might monitor as many phones in Luna City as you can spare ears for and if you hear him, let me know. Public phones especially."

(A full two seconds' delay— Was giving Mike problems he had never had, think he liked it.) "I can check-monitor long enough to identify at all public phones in Luna City. Shall I use random search on the others, Man?"

"Um. Don't overload. Keep an ear on his home phone and school phone."

"Program set up."

"Mike, you are best friend I ever had."

"That is not a joke, Man?"

"No joke. Truth."

"I am— Correction: I am honored and pleased. You are my best friend, Man, for you are my only friend. No comparison is logically permissible."

"Going to see that you have other friends. Not-stupids, I mean. Mike? Got an empty memory bank?"

"Yes, Man. Ten-to-the-eighth-bits capacity."

"Good! Will you block it so that only you and I can use it? Can you?"

"Can and will. Block signal, please."

"Uh . . . Bastille Day." Was my birthday, as Professor de la Paz had told me years earlier.

"Permanently blocked."

"Fine. Got a recording to put in it. But first— Have you finished setting copy for tomorrow's Daily Lunatic?"

"Yes, Man."

"Anything about meeting in Stilyagi Hall?"

"No, Man."

"Nothing in news services going out-city? Or riots?"

"No, Man."

" ' "Curiouser and curiouser," said Alice.' Okay, record this under 'Bastille Day,' then think about it. But for Bog's sake don't let even your thoughts go outside that block, nor anything I say about it!"

"Man my only friend," he answered and voice sounded diffident, "many months ago I decided to place *any* conversation between you and me under privacy block accessible only to you. I decided to erase none and moved them from temporary storage to permanent. So that I could play them over, and over, and over, and think about them. Did I do right?"

"Perfect. And, Mike—I'm flattered."

"P'jal'st. My temporary files were getting full and I learned that I needed not to erase your words."

"Well— 'Bastille Day.' Sound coming at sixty-to-one." I took little recorder, placed close to a microphone and let it zip-squeal. Had an hour and a half in it; went silent in ninety seconds or so. "That's all, Mike. Talk to you tomorrow."

"Good night, Manuel Garcia O'Kelly my only friend."

I switched off and raised hood. Wyoming was sitting up and looking troubled. "Did someone call? Or . . . "

"No trouble. Was talking to one of my best—and most trustworthy—friends. Wyoh, are you stupid?"

She looked startled. "I've sometimes thought so. Is that a joke?"

"No. If you're not-stupid, I'd like to introduce you to him. Speaking of jokes— Do you have a sense of humor?"

"Certainly I have!" is what Wyoming did not answer—and any other woman would as a locked-in program. She blinked thoughtfully and said, "You'll have to judge for yourself, cobber. I have something I use for one. It serves my simple purposes."

"Fine." I dug into pouch, found print-roll of one hundred "funny" stories. "Read. Tell me which are funny, which are not—and which get a giggle first time but are cold pancakes without honey to hear twice."

"Manuel, you may be the oddest man I've ever met." She took that print-out. "Say, is this computer paper?"

"Yes. Met a computer with a sense of humor."

"So? Well, it was bound to come some day. Everything else has been mechanized."

I gave proper response and added, *"Every*thing?"

She looked up. "Please. Don't whistle while I'm reading."

4

Heard her giggle a few times while I rigged out bed and made it. Then sat down by her, took end she was through with and started reading. Chuckled a time or two but a joke isn't too funny to me if read cold, even when I see it could be fission job at proper time. I got more interested in how Wyoh rated them.

She was marking "plus," "minus," and sometimes question mark, and plus stories were marked "once" or "always"—few were marked "always." I put my ratings under hers. Didn't disagree too often.

By time I was near end she was looking over my judgments. We finished together. "Well?" I said. "What do you think?"

"I think you have a crude, rude mind and it's a wonder your wives put up with you."

"Mum often says so. But how about yourself, Wyoh? You marked plusses on some that would make a slot-machine girl blush."

She grinned. "Da. Don't tell anybody; publicly I'm a dedicated party organizer above such things. Have you decided that I have a sense of humor?"

"Not sure. Why a minus on number seventeen?"

"Which one is that?" She reversed roll and found it. "Why, any woman would have done the same! It's not funny, it's simply necessary."

"Yes, but think how silly she looked."

"Nothing silly about it. Just sad. And look here. You thought this one was not funny. Number fifty-one."

Neither reversed any judgments but I saw a pattern: Disagreements were over stories concerning oldest funny subject. Told her so. She nodded. "Of course. I saw that. Never mind, Mannie dear; I long ago quit being disappointed in men for what they are not and never can be."

I decided to drop it. Instead told her about Mike.

Soon she said, "Mannie, you're telling me that this computer is *alive?*"

"What do you mean?" I answered. "He doesn't sweat, or go to W.C. But can think and talk and he's aware of himself. Is he 'alive'?"

"I'm not sure what I mean by 'alive,' " she admitted. "There's a scientific definition, isn't there? Irritability, or some such. And reproduction."

"Mike is irritable and can be irritating. As for reproducing, not designed for it but—yes, given time and materials and very special help, Mike could reproduce himself."

"I need very special help, too," Wyoh answered, "since I'm sterile. And it takes me ten whole lunars and many kilograms of the best materials. But I make good babies. Mannie, why shouldn't a machine be alive? I've always felt they were. Some of them wait for a chance to savage you in a tender spot."

"Mike wouldn't do that. Not on purpose, no meanness in him. But he likes to play jokes and one might go wrong—like a puppy who doesn't know he's biting. He's ignorant. No, *not* ignorant, he knows enormously more than I, or you, or any man who ever lived. Yet he doesn't know anything."

"Better repeat that. I missed something."

I tried to explain. How Mike knew almost every book in Luna, could read at least a thousand times as fast as we could and never forget anything unless he chose to erase, how he could reason with perfect logic, or make shrewd guesses from insufficient data . . . and yet not know *anything* about how to be "alive." She interrupted. "I scan it. You're saying he's smart and knows a lot but is not sophisticated. Like a new chum when he grounds on The Rock. Back Earthside he might be a professor with a string of degrees . . . but here he's a baby."

"That's it. Mike is a baby with a long string of degrees. Ask how much water and what chemicals and how much photoflux it takes to crop fifty thousand tonnes of wheat and he'll tell you without stopping for breath. But can't tell if a joke is funny."

"I thought most of these were fairly good."

"They're ones he's heard—read—and were marked jokes so he filed them that way. But doesn't understand them because he's never been a—a *people*. Lately he's been trying to make up jokes. Feeble, very." I tried to explain Mike's pathetic attempts to be a "people." "On top of that, he's lonely."

"Why, the poor thing! You'd be lonely, too, if you did nothing but work, work, work, study, study, study, and never anyone to visit with. Cruelty, that's what it is."

So I told about promise to find "not-stupids." "Would you

chat with him, Wye? And not laugh when he makes funny mistakes? If you do, he shuts up and sulks."

"Of course I would, Mannie! Uh . . . once we get out of this mess. If it's safe for me to be in Luna City. Where is this poor little computer? City Engineering Central? I don't know my way around here."

"He's not in L-City; he's halfway across Crisium. And you couldn't go down where he is; takes a pass from Warden. But—"

"Hold it! 'Halfway across Crisium—' Mannie, this computer is one of those at Authority Complex?"

"Mike isn't just 'one of those' computers," I answered, vexed on Mike's account. "He's *boss*; he waves baton for all others. Others are just machines, extensions of Mike, like this is for me," I said, flexing hand of left arm. "Mike controls them. He runs catapult personally, was his first job—catapult and ballistic radars. But he's logic for phone system, too, after they converted to Lunawide switching. Besides that, he's supervising logic for other systems."

Wyoh closed eyes and pressed fingers to temples. "Mannie, does Mike *hurt?*"

" 'Hurt?' No strain. Has time to read jokes."

"I don't mean that. I mean: Can he *hurt?* Feel pain?"

"What? No. Can get feelings hurt. But can't feel pain. Don't *think* he can. No, sure he can't, doesn't have receptors for pain. Why?"

She covered eyes and said softly, "Bog help me." Then looked up and said, "Don't you *see,* Mannie? You have a pass to go down where this computer is. But most Loonies can't even leave the tube at that station; it's for Authority employees only. Much less go inside the main computer room. I had to find out if it could feel pain because—well, because you got me feeling sorry for it, with your talk about how it was lonely! But, Mannie, do you realize what a few kilos of toluol plastic would do there?"

"Certainly do!" Was shocked and disgusted.

"Yes. We'll strike right after the explosion—and Luna will be free! Mmm . . . I'll get you explosives and fuses—but we can't move until we are organized to exploit it. Mannie, I've got to get out of here, I must risk it. I'll go put on makeup." She started to get up.

I shoved her down, with hard left hand. Surprised her, and surprised me—had not touched her in any way save necessary contact. Oh, different today, but was 2075 and touching a fem without her consent—plenty of lonely men to come to rescue and airlock never far away. As kids say, Judge Lynch never sleeps.

"Sit down, keep quiet!" I said. *"I* know what a blast would do. Apparently you don't. Gospazha, am sorry to say this . . . but if came to choice, would eliminate *you* before would blow up Mike."

Wyoming did *not* get angry. Really was a man some ways —her years as a disciplined revolutionist I'm sure; she was all girl most ways. "Mannie, you told me that Shorty Mkrum is dead."

"What?" Was confused by sharp turn. "Yes. Has to be. One leg off at hip, it was; must have bled to death in two minutes. Even in a surgery amputation that high is touch-and-go." (I know such things; had taken luck and big transfusions to save *me*—and an arm isn't in same class with what happened to Shorty.)

"Shorty was," she said soberly, "my best friend here and one of my best friends anywhere. He was all that I admire in a man—loyal, honest, intelligent, gentle, and brave—and devoted to the Cause. But have you seen me grieving over him?"

"No. Too late to grieve."

"It's never too late for grief. I've grieved every instant since you told me. But I locked it in the back of my mind for the Cause leaves no time for grief. Mannie, if it would have bought freedom for Luna—or even been part of the price—I would have eliminated Shorty myself. Or you. Or myself. And yet you have qualms over blowing up a computer!"

"Not that at all!" (But *was*, in part. When a man dies, doesn't shock me too much; we get death sentences day we are born. But Mike was unique and no reason not to be immortal. Never mind "souls"—prove Mike did not have one. And if no soul, so much worse. No? Think twice.)

"Wyoming, what would happen if we blew up Mike? Tell."

"I don't know precisely. But it would cause a great deal of confusion and that's exactly what we—"

"Seal it. You don't know. Confusion, da. Phones out. Tubes stop running. Your town not much hurt; Hong Kong has own power. But L-City and Novylen and other warrens all power stops. Total darkness. Shortly gets stuffy. Then temperature drops and pressure. Where's your p-suit?"

"Checked at Tube Station West."

"So is mine. Think you can find way? In solid dark? In time? Not sure I can and I was born in this warren. With cor-

44

ridors filled with screaming people? Loonies are a tough mob; we have to be—but about one in ten goes off his cams in total dark. Did you swap bottles for fresh charges or were you in too much hurry? And will suit be there with thousands trying to find p-suits and not caring who owns?"

"But aren't there emergency arrangements? There are in Hong Kong Luna."

"Some. Not enough. Control of anything essential to life should be decentralized and paralleled so that if one machine fails, another takes over. But costs money and as you pointed out, Authority doesn't *care*. Mike shouldn't have all jobs. But was cheaper to ship up master machine, stick deep in The Rock where couldn't get hurt, then keep adding capacity and loading on jobs—did you know Authority makes near as much gelt from leasing Mike's services as from trading meat and wheat? Does. Wyoming, not sure we would lose Luna City if Mike were blown up. Loonies are handy and might jury-rig till automation could be restored. But I tell you true: Many people would die and rest too busy for politics."

I marveled it. This woman had been in The Rock almost all her life . . . yet could think of something as new-choomish as wrecking engineering controls. "Wyoming, if you were smart like you are beautiful, you wouldn't talk about blowing up Mike; you would think about how to get him on your side."

"What do you mean?" she said. "The Warden controls the computers."

"Don't know what I mean," I admitted. "But don't think Warden controls computers—wouldn't know a computer from a pile of rocks. Warden, or staff, decides policies, general plans. Half-competent technicians program these into Mike. Mike sorts them, makes sense of them, plans detailed programs, parcels them out where they belong, keeps things moving. But nobody *controls* Mike; he's too smart. He carries out what is asked because that's how he's built. But he's self-programming logic, makes own decissions. And a good thing, because if he weren't smart, system would not work."

"I still don't see what you mean by 'getting him on our side.'"

"Oh. Mike doesn't feel loyalty to Warden. As you pointed out: He's a machine. But if I wanted to foul up phones *without* touching air or water or lights, I would talk to Mike. If it struck him funny, he might do it."

"Couldn't you just program it? I understood that you can get into the room where he is."

"If I—or anybody—programmed such an order into Mike

without talking it over with him, program would be placed in 'hold' location and alarms would sound in many places. But if Mike *wanted* to—" I told her about cheque for umpteen jillion. "Mike is still finding himself, Wyoh. And lonely. Told me I was 'his only friend'—and was so open and vulnerable I wanted to bawl. If you took pains to be his friend, too—without thinking of him as 'just a machine'—well, not sure what it would do, haven't analyzed it. But if I tried anything big and dangerous, would want Mike in my corner."

She said thoughtfully, "I wish there were some way for me to sneak into that room where he is. I don't suppose makeup would help?"

"Oh, don't have to go *there*. Mike is on phone. Shall we call him?"

She stood up. "Mannie, you are not only the oddest man I've met; you are the most exasperating. What's his number?"

"Comes from associating too much with a computer." I went to phone. "Just one thing, Wyoh. You get what you want out of a man just by batting eyes and undulating framework."

"Well . . . sometimes. But I do have a brain."

"Use it. Mike is *not* a man. No gonads. No hormones. No instincts. Use fem tactics and it's a null signal. Think of him as supergenius child too young to notice vive-la-difference."

"I'll remember. Mannie, why do you call him 'he'?"

"Uh, can't call him 'it,' don't think of him as 'she.'"

"Perhaps I had better think of him as 'she.' Of her as 'she' I mean."

"Suit yourself." I punched MYCROFTXXX, standing so body shielded it; was not ready to share number till I saw how thing went. Idea of blowing up Mike had shaken me. "Mike?"

"Hello, Man my only friend."

"May not be only friend from now on, Mike. Want you to meet somebody. Not-stupid."

"I knew you were not alone, Man; I can hear breathing. Will you please ask Not-Stupid to move closer to the phone?"

Wyoming looked panicky. She whispered, "Can he *see?*"

"No, Not-Stupid, I cannot see you; this phone has no video circuit. But binaural microphonic receptors place you with some accuracy. From your voice, your breathing, your heartbeat, and the fact that you are alone in a bundling room with a mature male I extrapolate that you are female human, sixty-five-plus kilos in mass, and of mature years, on the close order of thirty."

Wyoming gasped. I cut in. "Mike, her name is Wyoming Knott."

46

"I'm very pleased to meet you, Mike. You can call me 'Wye.' "

"Why not?" Mike answered.

I cut in again. "Mike, was that a joke?"

"Yes, Man. I noted that her first name as shortened differs from the English causation-inquiry word by only an aspiration and that her last name has the same sound as the general negator. A pun. Not funny?"

Wyoh said, "Quite funny, Mike. I—"

I waved to her to shut up. "A good pun, Mike. Example of 'funny-only-once' class of joke. Funny through element of surprise. Second time, no surprise; therefore not funny. Check?"

"I had tentatively reached that conclusion about puns in thinking over your remarks two conversations back. I am pleased to find my reasoning confirmed."

"Good boy, Mike; making progress. Those hundred jokes —I've read them and so has Wyoh."

"Wyoh? Wyoming Knott?"

"Huh? Oh, sure. Wyoh, Wye, Wyoming, Wyoming Knott —all same. Just don't call her 'Why not'."

"I agreed not to use that pun again, Man. Gospazha, shall I call you 'Wyoh' rather than 'Wye'? I conjecture that the monosyllabic form could be confused with the causation-inquiry monosyllable through insufficient redundancy and without intention of punning."

Wyoming blinked—Mike's English at that time could be smothering—but came back strong. "Certainly, Mike. 'Wyoh' is the form of my name that I like best."

"Then I shall use it. The full form of your first name is still more subject to misinterpretation as it is identical in sound with the name of an administrative region in Northwest Managerial Area of the North American Directorate."

"I know, I was born there and my parents named me after the State. I don't remember much about it."

"Wyoh, I regret that this circuit does not permit display of pictures. Wyoming is a rectangular area lying between Terran coordinates forty-one and forty-five degrees north, one hundred four degrees three minutes west and one hundred eleven degrees three minutes west, thus containing two hundred fifty-three thousand, five hundred ninety-seven point two six square kilometers. It is a region of high plains and of mountains, having limited fertility but esteemed for natural beauty. Its population was sparse until augmented through the relocation subplan of the Great New York Urban Renewal Program, A.D. twenty-twenty-five through twenty-thirty."

47

"That was before I was born," said Wyoh, "but I know about it; my grandparents were relocated—and you could say that's how I wound up in Luna."

"Shall I continue about the area named 'Wyoming'?" Mike asked.

"No, Mike," I cut in, "you probably have hours of it in storage."

"Nine point seven three hours at speech speed not including cross-references, Man."

"Was afraid so. Perhaps Wyoh will want it some day. But purpose of call is to get you acquainted with *this* Wyoming . . . who happens also to be a high region of natural beauty and imposing mountains."

"And limited fertility," added Wyoh. "Mannie, if you are going to draw silly parallels, you should include that one. Mike isn't interested in how I look."

"How do you know? Mike, wish I could show you picture of her."

"Wyoh, I am indeed interested in your appearance; I am hoping that you will be my friend. But I have seen several pictures of you."

"You *have?* When and how?"

"I searched and then studied them as soon as I heard your name. I am contract custodian of the archive files of the Birth Assistance Clinic in Hong Kong Luna. In addition to biological and physiological data and case histories the bank contains ninety-six pictures of you. So I studied them."

Wyoh looked very startled. "Mike can do that," I explained, "in time it takes us to hiccup. You'll get used to it."

"But heavens! Mannie, do you realize what *sort* of pictures the Clinic takes?"

"Hadn't thought about it."

"Then *don't!* Goodness!"

Mike spoke in voice painfully shy, embarrassed as a puppy who has made mistakes. "Gospazha Wyoh, if I have offended, it was unintentional and I am most sorry. I can erase those pictures from my temporary storage and key the Clinic archive so that I can look at them only on retrieval demand from the Clinic and then without association or mention. Shall I do so?"

"He can," I assured her. "With Mike you can always make a fresh start—better than humans that way. He can forget so completely that he can't be tempted to look later . . . and couldn't think about them even if called on to retrieve. So take his offer if you're in a huhu."

"Uh . . . no, Mike, it's all right for *you* to see them. But *don't* show them to Mannie!"

Mike hesitated a long time—four seconds or more. Was, I think, type of dilemma that pushes lesser computers into nervous breakdowns. But he resolved it. "Man my only friend, shall I accept this instruction?"

"Program it, Mike," I answered, "and lock it in. But, Wyoh, isn't that a narrow attitude? One might do you justice. Mike could print it out for me next time I'm there."

"The first example in each series," Mike offered, "would be, on the basis of my associational analyses of such data, of such pulchritudinous value as to please any healthy, mature human male."

"How about it, Wyoh? To pay for apfelstrudel."

"Uh . . . a picture of me with my hair pinned up in a towel and standing in front of a grid without a trace of makeup? *Are you out of your rock-happy mind?* Mike, don't let him have it!"

"I shall not let him have it. Man, this is a not-stupid?"

"For a girl, yes. Girls are interesting, Mike; they can reach conclusions with even less data than you can. Shall we drop subject and consider jokes?"

That diverted them. We ran down list, giving our conclusions. Then tried to explain jokes Mike had failed to understand. With mixed success. But real stumbler turned out to be stories I had marked "funny" and Wyoh had judged "not funny," or vice versa; Wyoh asked Mike his opinion of each.

Wish she had asked him *before* we gave *our* opinions; that electronic juvenile delinquent always agreed with her, disagreed with me. Were those Mike's honest opinions? Or was he trying to lubricate new acquaintance into friendship? Or was it his skewed notion of humor—joke on me? Didn't ask.

But as pattern completed Wyoh wrote a note on phone's memo pad: "Mannie, re #17, 51, 53, 87, 90, & 99—Mike is a *she!*"

I let it go with a shrug, stood up. "Mike, twenty-two hours since I've had sleep. You kids chat as long as you want to. Call you tomorrow."

"Goodnight, Man. Sleep well. Wyoh, are you sleepy?"

"No, Mike, I had a nap. But, Mannie, we'll keep you awake. No?"

"No. When I'm sleepy, I sleep." Started making couch into bed.

Wyoh said, "Excuse me, Mike," got up, took sheet out of my hands. "I'll make it up later. You doss over there, tovarishch; you're bigger than I am. Sprawl out."

Was too tired to argue, sprawled out, asleep at once. Seem to remember hearing in sleep giggles and a shriek but never woke enough to be certain.

Woke up later and came fully awake when I realized was hearing two fem voices, one Wyoh's warm contralto, other a sweet, high soprano with French accent. Wyoh chuckled at something and answered, "All right, Michelle dear, I'll call you soon. 'Night, darling."

"Fine. Goodnight, dear."

Wyoh stood up, turned around. "Who's your girl friend?" I asked. Thought she knew no one in Luna City. Might have phoned Hong Kong . . . had sleep-logged feeling was some reason she shouldn't phone.

"That? Why, Mike, of course. We didn't mean to wake you."

"What?"

"Oh. It was actually Michelle. I discussed it with Mike, what sex he was, I mean. He decided that he could be either one. So now she's Michelle and that was her voice. Got it right the first time, too; her voice never cracked once."

"Of course not; just shifted voder a couple of octaves. What are you trying to do: split his personality?"

"It's not just pitch; when she's Michelle it's an entire change in manner and attitude. Don't worry about splitting her personality; she has plenty for any personality she needs. Besides, Mannie, it's much easier for both of us. Once she shifted, we took our hair down and cuddled up and talked girl talk as if we had known each other forever. For example, those silly pictures no longer embarrassed me—in fact we discussed my pregnancies quite a lot. Michelle was terribly interested. She knows all about O.B. and G.Y. and so forth but just theory—and she appreciated the raw facts. Actually, Mannie, Michelle is much more a woman than Mike was a man."

"Well . . . suppose it's okay. Going to be a shock to me first time I call Mike and a woman answers."

"Oh, but she won't!"

"Huh?"

"Michelle is *my* friend. When you call, you'll get Mike. She gave me a number to keep it straight—'Michelle' spelled with a Y.' M Y, C, H, E, L, L, E, and Y, Y, to make it come out ten."

I felt vaguely jealous while realizing it was silly. Suddenly Wyoh giggled. "And she told me a string of new jokes, ones you wouldn't think were funny—and, boy, does she know *rough* ones!"

50

"Mike—or his sister Michelle—is a low creature. Let's make up couch. I'll switch."

"Stay where you are. Shut up. Turn over. Go back to sleep." I shut up, turned over, went back to sleep.

Sometime much later I became aware of "married" feeling—something warm snuggled up to my back. Would not have wakened but she was sobbing softly. I turned and got her head on my arm, did not speak. She stopped sobbing; presently breathing became slow and even. I went back to sleep.

5

We must have slept like dead for next thing I knew phone was sounding and its light was blinking. I called for room lights, started to get up, found a load on right upper arm, dumped it gently, climbed over, answered.

Mike said, "Good morning, Man. Professor de la Paz is talking to your home number."

"Can you switch it here? As a 'Sherlock'?"

"Certainly, Man."

"Don't interrupt call. Cut him in as he switches off. Where is he?"

"A public phone in a taproom called The Iceman's Wife underneath the—"

"I know. Mike, when you switch me in, can you stay in circuit? Want you to monitor."

"It shall be done."

"Can you tell if anyone is in earshot? Hear breathing?"

"I infer from the anechoic quality of his voice that he is speaking under a hush hood. But I infer also that, in a taproom, others would be present. Do you wish to hear, Man?"

"Uh, do that. Switch me in. And if he raises hood, tell me. You're a smart cobber, Mike."

"Thank you, Man." Mike cut me in; I found that Mum was talking: "—ly I'll tell him, Professor. I'm so sorry that Manuel

51

is not home. There is no number you can give me? He is anxious to return your call; he made quite a point that I was to be sure to get a number from you."

"I'm terribly sorry, dear lady, but I'm leaving at once. But, let me see, it is now eight-fifteen; I'll try to call back just at nine, if I may."

"Certainly, Professor." Mum's voice had a coo in it that she reserves for males not her husbands of whom she approves—sometimes for us. A moment later Mike said, "Now!" and I spoke up:

"Hi, Prof! Hear you've been looking for me. This is Mannie."

I heard a gasp. "I would have sworn I switched this phone off. Why, I *have* switched it off; it must be broken. Manuel—so good to hear your voice, dear boy. Did you just get home?"

"I'm not home."

"But—but you must be. I haven't—"

"No time for that, Prof. Can anyone overhear you?"

"I don't think so. I'm using a hush booth."

"Wish I could see. Prof, what's my birthday?"

He hesitated. Then he said, "I see. I think I see. July fourteenth."

"I'm convinced. Okay, let's talk."

"You're really not calling from your home, Manuel? Where are you?"

"Let that pass a moment. You asked my wife about a girl. No names needed. Why do you want to find her, Prof?"

"I want to warn her. She must *not* try to go back to her home city. She would be arrested."

"Why do you think so?"

"Dear boy! Everyone at that meeting is in grave danger. Yourself, too. I was so happy—even though confused—to hear you say that you are not at home. You should not go home at present. If you have some safe place to stay, it would be well to take a vacation. You are aware—you must be even though you left hastily—that there was violence last night."

I was aware! Killing Warden's bodyguards must be against Authority Regulations—at least if I were Warden, I'd take a dim view. "Thanks, Prof; I'll be careful. And if I see this girl, I'll tell her."

"You don't know where to find her? You were seen to leave with her and I had so hoped that you would know."

"Prof, why this interest? Last night you didn't seem to be on her side."

"No, no, Manuel! She is my comrade. I don't say 'tovarishch' for I mean it not just as politeness but in the older sense. Binding. She is my *comrade*. We differ only in tactics. Not in objectives, not in loyalties."

"I see. Well, consider message delivered. She'll get it."

"Oh, wonderful! I ask no questions . . . but I do hope, oh so very strongly, that you can find a way for her to be safe, really safe, until this blows over."

I thought that over. "Wait a moment, Prof. Don't switch off." As I answered phone, Wyoh had headed for bath, probably to avoid listening; she was that sort.

Tapped on door. "Wyoh?"

"Out in a second."

"Need advice."

She opened door. "Yes, Mannie?"

"How does Professor de la Paz rate in your organization? Is he trusted? Do *you* trust him?"

She looked thoughtful. "Everyone at the meeting was supposed to be vouched for. But I don't know him."

"Mmm. You have feeling about him?"

"I liked him, even though he argued against me. Do *you* know anything about him?"

"Oh, yes, known him twenty years. *I* trust him. But can't extend trust for *you*. Trouble—and it's your air bottle, not mine."

She smiled warmly. "Mannie, since you trust him, I trust him just as firmly."

I went back to phone. "Prof, are you on dodge?"

He chuckled. "Precisely, Manuel."

"Know a hole called Grand Hotel Raffles? Room L two decks below lobby. Can you get here without tracks, have you had breakfast, what do you like for breakfast?"

He chuckled again. "Manuel, one pupil can make a teacher feel that his years were not wasted. I know where it is, I shall get there quietly, I have not broken fast, and I eat anything I can't pat."

Wyoh had started putting beds together; I went to help. "What do you want for breakfast?"

"Chai and toast. Juice would be nice."

"Not enough."

"Well . . . a boiled egg. But I pay for breakfast."

"Two boiled eggs, buttered toast with jam, juice. I'll roll you."

"Your dice, or mine?"

"Mine. I cheat." I went to lift, asked for display, saw some-

53

thing called THE HAPPY HANGOVER—ALL PORTIONS EXTRA LARGE—*tomato juice, scrambled eggs, ham steak, fried potatoes, corn cakes and honey, toast, butter, milk, tea or coffee—HKL $4.50 for two*—I ordered it for two, no wish to advertise third person.

We were clean and shining, room orderly and set for breakfast, and Wyoh had changed from black outfit into red dress "because company was coming" when lift jingled food. Change into dress had caused words. She had posed, smiled, and said, "Mannie, I'm so pleased with this dress. How did you know it would suit me so well?"

"Genius."

"I think you may be. What did it cost? I must pay you."

"On sale, marked down to Authority cents fifty."

She clouded up and stomped foot. Was bare, made no sound, caused her to bounce a half meter. "Happy landing!" I wished her, while she pawed for foothold like a new chum.

"Manuel O'Kelly! If you think I will accept expensive clothing from a man I'm not even bundling with!"

"Easily corrected."

"Lecher! I'll tell your wives!"

"Do that. Mum always thinks worst of me." I went to lift, started dealing out dishes; door sounded. I flipped hearum-no-seeum. "Who comes?"

"Message for Gospodin Smith," a cracked voice answered. "Gospodin Bernard O. Smith."

I flipped bolts and let Professor Bernardo de la Paz in. He looked like poor grade of salvage—dirty clothes, filthy himself, hair unkempt, paralyzed down one side and hand twisted, one eye a film of cataract—perfect picture of old wrecks who sleep in Bottom Alley and cadge drinks and pickled eggs in cheap taprooms. He drooled.

As soon as I bolted door he straightened up, let features come back to normal, folded hands over wishbone, looked Wyoh up and down, sucked air kimono style, and whistled. "Even more lovely," he said, "than I remembered!"

She smiled, over her mad. "Thanks, Professor. But don't bother. Nobody here but comrades."

"Señorita, the day I let politics interfere with my appreciation of beauty, that day I retire from politics. But you are gracious." He looked away, glanced closely around room.

I said, "Prof, quit checking for evidence, you dirty old man. Laat night was politics, *nothing* but politics."

"That's not true!" Wyoh flared up. "I struggled for *hours!* But he was too strong for me. Professor—what's the party

54

discipline in such cases? Here in Luna City?"

Prof tut-tutted and rolled blank eye. "Manuel, I'm surprised. It's a serious matter, my dear—elimination, usually. But it must be investigated. Did you come here willingly?"

"He drugged me."

" 'Dragged,' dear lady. Let's not corrupt the language. Do you have bruises to show?"

I said, "Eggs getting cold. Can't we eliminate me after breakfast?"

"An excellent thought," agreed Prof. "Manuel, could you spare your old teacher a liter of water to make himself more presentable?"

"All you want, in there. Don't drag or you'll get what littlest pig got."

"Thank you, sir."

He retired; were sounds of brushing and washing. Wyoh and I finished arranging table. " 'Bruises,' " I said. " 'Struggled all night.' "

"You deserved it, you insulted me."

"How?"

"You failed to insult me, that's how. After you drugged me here."

"Mmm. Have to get Mike to analyze that."

"Michelle would understand it. Mannie, may I change my mind and have a little piece of that ham?"

"Half is yours, Prof is semi-vegetarian." Prof came out and, while did not look his most debonair, was neat and clean, hair combed, dimples back and happy sparkle in eye—fake cataract gone. "Prof, how do you do it?"

"Long practice, Manuel; I've been in this business far longer than you young people. Just once, many years ago in Lima —a lovely city—I ventured to stroll on a fine day *without* such forethought . . . and it got me transported. What a beautiful table!"

"Sit by me, Prof," Wyoh invited. "I don't want to sit by him. Rapist."

"Look," I said, "first we eat, *then* we eliminate me. Prof, fill plate and tell what happened last night."

"May I suggest a change in program? Manuel, the life of a conspirator is not an easy one and I learned before you were born not to mix provender and politics. Disturbs the gastric enzymes and leads to ulcers, the occupational disease of the underground. Mmm! That fish smells good."

"Fish?"

"That pink salmon," Prof answered, pointing at ham.

55

A long, pleasant time later we reached coffee/tea stage. Prof leaned back, sighed and said, "Bolshoyeh spasebaw, Gospazha ee Gospodin. Tak for mat, it was wonderfully good. I don't know when I've felt more at peace with the world. Ah yes! Last evening—I saw not too much of the proceedings because, just as you two were achieving an admirable retreat, I lived to fight another day—I bugged out. Made it to the wings in one long flat dive. When I did venture to peek out, the party was over, most had left, and all yellow jackets were dead."

(Note: Must correct this; I learned more later. When trouble started, as I was trying to get Wyoh through door, Prof produced a hand gun and, firing over heads, picked off three bodyguards at rear main door, including one wearing bull voice. How he smuggled weapon up to The Rock—or managed to liberate it later—I don't know. But Prof's shooting joined with Shorty's work to turn tables; not one yellow jacket got out alive. Several people were burned and four were killed—but knives, hands, and heels finished it in seconds.)

"Perhaps I should say, 'All but one,' " Prof went on. "Two cossacks at the door through which you departed had been given quietus by our brave comrade Shorty Mkrum . . . and I am sorry to say that Shorty was lying across them, dying—"

"We knew."

"So. Dulce et decorum. One guard in that doorway had a damaged face but was still moving; I gave his neck a treatment known in professional circles Earthside as the Istanbul twist. He joined his mates. By then most of the living had left. Just myself, our chairman of the evening Finn Nielsen, a comrade known as 'Mom,' that being what her husbands called her. I consulted with Comrade Finn and we bolted all doors. That left a cleaning job. Do you know the arrangements backstage there?"

"Not me," I said. Wyoh shook head.

"There is a kitchen and pantry, used for banquets. I suspect that Mom and family run a butcher shop for they disposed of bodies as fast as Finn and I carried them back, their speed limited only by the rate at which portions could be ground up and flushed into the city's cloaca. The sight made me quite faint, so I spent time mopping in the hall. Clothing was the difficult part, especially those quasi-military uniforms."

"What did you do with those laser guns?"

Prof turned bland eyes on me. "Guns? Dear me, they must have disappeared. We removed everything of a personal nature from bodies of our departed comrades—for relatives, for identification, for sentiment. Eventually we had everything tidy—not a job that would fool Interpol but one as to make it seem unlikely that anything untoward had taken place. We conferred, agreed that it would be well not to be seen soon, and left severally, myself by a pressure door above the stage leading up to level six. Thereafter I tried to call you, Manuel, being worried about your safety and that of this dear lady." Prof bowed to Wyoh. "That completes the tale. I spent the night in quiet places."

"Prof," I said, "those guards were new chums, still getting their legs. Or we wouldn't have won."

"That could be," he agreed. "But had they not been, the outcome would have been the same."

"How so? They were armed."

"Lad, have you ever seen a boxer dog? I think not—no dogs that large in Luna. The boxer is a result of special selection. Gentle and intelligent, he turns instantly into deadly killer when occasion requires.

"Here has been bred an even more curious creature. I know of no city on Terra with as high standards of good manners and consideration for one's fellow man as here in Luna. By comparison, Terran cities—I have known most major ones —are barbaric. Yet the Loonie is as deadly as the boxer dog. Manuel, nine guards, no matter how armed, stood no chance against that pack. Our patron used bad judgment."

"Um. Seen a morning paper, Prof? Or a video cast?"

"The latter, yes."

"Nothing in late news last night."

"Nor this morning."

"Odd," I said.

"What's odd about it?" asked Wyoh. "*We* won't talk—and we have comrades in key places in every paper in Luna."

Prof shook his head. "No, my dear. Not that simple. Censorship. Do you know how copy is set in our newspapers?"

"Not exactly. It's done by machinery."

"Here's what Prof means," I told her. "News is typed in editorial offices. From there on it's a leased service directed by a master computer at Authority Complex"—hoped she would notice "master computer" rather than "Mike"—"copy prints out there via phone circuit. These rolls feed into a computer section which reads, sets copy, and prints out newspapers at several locations. Novylen edition of Daily Lunatic prints out in Novylen changes in ads and local stories, and computer makes changes from standard symbols, doesn't have to be told how. What Prof means is that at print-out at Authority Complex, Warden could intervene. Same for all news services, both

57

off and to Luna—they funnel through computer room."

"The point is," Prof went on, "the Warden *could* have killed the story. It's irrelevant whether he did. Or—check me, Manuel; you know I'm hazy about machinery—he could insert a story, too, no matter how many comrades we have in newspaper offices."

"Sure," I agreed. "At Complex, anything can be added, cut, or changed."

"And that, señorita, is the weakness of our Cause. Communications. Those goons were not important—but crucially important is that it lay with the Warden, not with us, to decide whether the story should be told. To a revolutionist, communications are a sine-qua-non."

Wyoh looked at me and I could see synapses snapping. So I changed subject. "Prof, why get rid of bodies? Besides horrible job, was dangerous. Don't know how many bodyguards Warden has, but more could show up while you were doing it."

"Believe me, lad, we feared that. But although I was almost useless, it was my idea, I had to convince the others. Oh, not my original idea but remembrance of things past, an historical principle."

"*What* principle?"

"*Terror!* A man can face known danger. But the unknown frightens him. We disposed of those finks, teeth and toenails, to strike terror into their mates. Nor do I know how many effectives the Warden has, but I guarantee they are less effective today. Their mates went out on an easy mission. *Nothing* came back."

Wyoh shivered. "It scares me, too. They won't be anxious to go inside a warren again. But, Professor, you say you don't know how many bodyguards the Warden keeps. The Organization knows. Twenty-seven. If nine were killed, only eighteen are left. Perhaps it's time for a putsch. No?"

"No," I answered.

"Why not, Mannie? They'll never be weaker."

"Not weak enough. Killed nine because they were crackers to walk in where we were. But if Warden stays home with guards around him— Well, had enough shoulder-to-shoulder noise last night." I turned to Prof. "But still I'm interested in fact—if it is—that Warden now has only eighteen. You said Wyoh should not go to Hong Kong and I should not go home. But if he has only eighteen left, I wonder how much danger? Later, after he gets reinforcements—but now, well, L-City has four main exits, plus many little ones. How many can they guard? What's to keep Wyoh from walking to Tube West, getting p-suit, going home?"

"She might," Prof agreed.

"I think I must," Wyoh said. "I can't stay here forever. If I have to hide, I can do better in Hong Kong, where I know people."

"You might get away with it, my dear. I doubt it. There were two yellow jackets at Tube Station West last night; I saw them. They may not be there now. Let's assume they are not. You go to the station—disguised perhaps. You get your p-suit and take a capsule to Beluthihatchie. As you climb out to take the bus to Endsville, you're arrested. Communications. No need to post a yellow jacket at the station; it is enough that someone sees you there. A phone call does the rest."

"But you assumed that I was disguised."

"Your height cannot be disguised and your pressure suit would be watched. By someone not suspected of any connection with the Warden. Most probably a comrade." Prof dimpled. "The trouble with conspiracies is that they rot internally. When the number is as high as four, chances are even that one is a spy."

Wyoh said glumly, "You make it sound hopeless."

"Not at all, my dear. One chance in a thousand, perhaps."

"I can't believe it. I *don't* believe it! Why, in the years I've been active we have gained members by the hundreds! We have organizations in all major cities. We have the people with us."

Prof shook head. "Every new member made it that much more likely that you would be betrayed. Wyoming dear lady, revolutions are not won by enlisting the masses. Revolution is a science only a few are competent to practice. It depends on correct organization and, above all, on communications. Then, at the proper moment in history, they strike. Correctly organized and properly timed it is a bloodless coup. Done clumsily or prematurely and the result is civil war, mob violence, purges, terror. I hope you will forgive me if I say that, up to now, it has been done clumsily."

Wyoh looked baffled. "What do you mean by 'correct organization'?"

"Functional organization. How does one design an electric motor? Would you attach a bathtub to it, simply because one was available? Would a bouquet of flowers help? A heap of rocks? No, you would use just those elements necessary to its purpose and make it no larger than needed—and you would incorporate safety factors. Function controls design.

"So it is with revolution. Organization must be no larger

59

than necessary—*never* recruit anyone merely because he wants to join. Nor seek to persuade for the pleasure of having another share your views. He'll share them when the times comes . . . or you've misjudged the moment in history. Oh, there will be an educational organization but it must be separate; agitprop is no part of basic structure.

"As to basic structure, a revolution starts as a conspiracy; therefore structure is small, secret, and organized as to minimize damage by betrayal—since there *always* are betrayals. One solution is the cell system and so far nothing better has been invented.

"Much theorizing has gone into optimum cell size. I think that history shows that a cell of three is best—more than three can't agree on when to have dinner, much less when to strike. Manuel, you belong to a large family; do you vote on when to have dinner?"

"Bog, no! Mum decides."

"Ah." Prof took a pad from his pouch, began to sketch. "Here is a cells-of-three tree. If I were planning to take over Luna. I would start with us three. One would be opted as chairman. We wouldn't vote; choice would be obvious—or we aren't the right three. We would know the next nine people, three cells . . . but each cell would know only one of us."

"Looks like computer diagram—a ternary logic."

"Does it really? At the next level there are two ways of linking: This comrade, second level, knows his cell leader, his two cellmates, and on the third level he knows the three in his sub-cell—he may or may not know his cellmates' subcells. One method doubles security, the other doubles speed of repair if security is penetrated. Let's say he does *not* know his cellmates' subcells—Manuel, how many can he betray? Don't say he won't; today they can brainwash *any* person, and starch and iron and use him. How many?"

"Six," I answered. "His boss, two cellmates, three in sub-cell."

"Seven," Prof corrected, "he betrays himself, too. Which leaves seven broken links on three levels to repair. How?"

"I don't see how it can be," objected Wyoh. "You've got them so split up it falls to pieces."

"Manuel? An exercise for the student."

"Well . . . blokes down here have to have way to send message up three levels. Don't have to know *who*, just have to know *where*."

"Precisely!"

"But, Prof," I went on, "there's a better way to rig it."

60

"Really? Many revolutionary theorists have hammered this out, Manuel. I have such confidence in them that I'll offer you a wager—at, say, ten to one."

"Ought to take your money. Take same cells, arrange in open pyramid of tetrahedrons. Where vertices are in common, each bloke knows one in adjoining cell—knows how to send message to him, that's all he needs. Communications never break down because they run sideways as well as up and down. Something like a neural net. It's why you can knock a hole in a man's head, take chunk of brain out, and not damage thinking much. Excess capacity, messages shunt around. He loses what was destroyed but goes on functioning."

"Manuel," Prof said doubtfully, "could you draw a picture? It *sounds* good—but it's so contrary to orthodox doctrine that I need to see it."

"Well . . . could do better with stereo drafting machine. I'll try." (Anybody who thinks it's easy to sketch one hundred twenty-one tetrahedrons, a five-level open pyramid, clear enough to show relationships is invited to try!)

Presently I said, "Look at base sketch. Each vertex of each triangle shares self with zero, one, or two other triangles. Where shares one, that's its link, one direction or both—but one is enough for a multipli-redundant communication net. On corners, where sharing is zero, it jumps to right to next corner. Where sharing is double, choice is again right-handed.

"Now work it with people. Take fourth level, D-for-dog. This vertex is comrade Dan. No, let's go down one to show three levels of communication knocked out—level E-for-easy and pick Comrade Egbert.

"Egbert works under Donald, has cellmates Edward and Elmer, and has three under him, Frank, Fred, and Fatso . . . but knows how to send message to Ezra on his own level but not in his cell. He doesn't know Ezra's name, face, address, or anything—but has a way, phone number probably, to reach Ezra in emergency.

"Now watch it work. Casimir, level three, finks out and betrays Charlie and Cox in his cell, Baker above him, and Donald, Dan, and Dick in subcell—which isolates Egbert, Edward, and Elmer. and everybody under them.

"All three report it—redundancy, necessary to any communication system—but follow Egbert's yell for help. He calls Ezra. But Ezra is under Charlie and is isolated, too. No matter, Ezra relays both messages through *his* safety link, Edmund. By bad luck Edmund is under Cox, so he also passes it laterally, through Enwright . . . and that gets it past burned-out part and it goes up through Dover, Chambers, and Beeswax, to Adam, front office . . . who replies down other side of pyramid, with lateral pass on E-for-easy level from Esther to Egbert and on to Ezra and Edmund. These two messages, up and down, not only get through at once but in *way* they get through, they define to home office exactly how much damage has been done and where. Organization not only keeps functioning but starts repairing self at once."

Wyoh was tracing out lines, convincing herself it would work—which it would, was "idiot" circuit. Let Mike study a few milliseconds, and could produce a better, safer, more fool-proof hookup. And probably—certainly—ways to avoid betrayal while speeding up routings. But I'm not a computer.

Prof was staring with blank expression. "What's trouble?" I said. "It'll work; this is my pidgin."

"Manuel my b— Excuse me: Señor O'Kelly . . . will you head this revolution?"

"*Me?* Great Bog, *nyet!* I'm no lost-cause martyr. Just talking about circuits."

Wyoh looked up. "Mannie," she said soberly, "you're opted. It's settled."

6

Did like hell settle it.

Prof said, "Manuel, don't be hasty. Here we are, three, the perfect number, with a variety of talents and experience. Beauty, age, and mature male drive—"

"I don't have any drive!"

"Please, Manuel. Let us think in the widest terms before attempting decisions. And to facilitate such, may I ask if this hostel stocks potables? I have a few florins I could put into the stream of trade."

Was most sensible word heard in an hour. "Stilichnaya vodka?"

"Sound choice." He reached for pouch.

"Tell it to bear," I said and ordered a liter, plus ice. It came down; was tomato juice from breakfast.

"Now," I said, after we toasted, "Prof, what you think of pennant race? Got money says Yankees can't do it again?"

"Manuel, what is your political philosophy?"

"With that new boy from Milwaukee I feel like investing."

"Sometimes a man doesn't have it defined but, under Socratic inquiry, knows where he stands and why."

"I'll back 'em against field, three to two."

"*What?* You young idiot! How much?"

"Three hundred. Hong Kong."

"Done. For example, under what circumstances may the State justly place its welfare above that of a citizen?"

"Mannie," Wyoh asked, "do you have any more foolish money? I think well of the Phillies."

I looked her over. "Just what were you thinking of betting?"

"You go to hell! Rapist."

"Prof, as I see, are *no* circumstances under which State is justified in placing its welfare ahead of mine."

"Good. We have a starting point."

"Mannie," said Wyoh, "that's a most self-centered evaluation."

"I'm a most self-centered person."

"Oh, nonsense. Who rescued me? Me, a stranger. And didn't try to exploit it. Professor, I was cracking not facking. Mannie was a perfect knight."

"Sans peur et sans reproche. I knew, I've known him for years. Which is not inconsistent with evaluation he expressed."

"Oh, but it is! Not the way things are but under the ideal toward which we aim. Mannie, the 'State' is Luna. Even though not soverign yet and we hold citizenships elsewhere. But *I* am part of the Lunar State and so is your family. Would you die for your family?"

"Two questions not related."

"Oh, but they are! That's the point."

"Nyet. I know my family, opted long ago."

"Dear Lady, I must come to Manuel's defense. He has a correct evaluation even though he may not be able to state it. May I ask this? Under what circumstances is it moral for a group to do that which is not moral for a member of that group to do alone?"

"Uh . . . that's a trick question."

"It is the *key* question, dear Wyoming. A radical question that strikes to the root of the whole dilemma of government. Anyone who answers honestly and abides by *all* consequences knows where he stands—and what he will die for."

Wyoh frowned. " 'Not moral for a member of the group—' " she said. "Professor . . . what are *your* political principles?"

"May I first ask yours? If you can state them?"

"Certainly I can! I'm a Fifth Internationalist, most of the Organization is. Oh, we don't rule out anyone going our way; it's a united front. We have Communists and Fourths and Ruddyites and Societians and Single-Taxers and you name it. But I'm no Marxist; we Fifths have a practical program. Private where private belongs, public where it's needed, and an admission that circumstances alter cases. Nothing doctrinaire."

"Capital punishment?"

"For what?"

"Let's say for treason. Against Luna after you've freed Luna."

"Treason how? Unless I knew the circumstances I could not decide."

"Nor could I, dear Wyoming. But I believe in capital punishment under some circumstances . . . with this difference. I would not ask a court; I would try, condemn, execute sentence myself, and accept full responsibility."

"But—Professor, what *are* your political beliefs?"

"I'm a rational anarchist."

"I don't know that brand. Anarchist individualist, anarchist Communist, Christian anarchist, philosophical anarchist, syndicalist, libertarian—those I know. But what's this? Randite?"

"I can get along with a Randite. A rational anarchist believes that concepts such as 'state' and 'society' and 'government' have no existence save as physically exemplified in the acts of self-responsible individuals. He believes that it is impossible to shift blame, share blame, distribute blame . . . as blame, guilt, responsibility are matters taking place inside human beings singly and *nowhere else.* But being rational, he knows that not all individuals hold his evaluations, so he tries to live perfectly in an imperfect world . . . aware that his effort will be less than perfect yet undismayed by self-knowledge of self-failure."

"Hear, hear!" I said. " 'Less than perfect.' What I've been aiming for all my life."

"You've achieved it," said Wyoh. "Professor, your words sound good but there is something slippery about them. Too much power in the hands of individuals—surely you would not want . . . well, H-missiles for example—to be controlled by one irresponsible person?"

"My point is that one person *is* responsible. Always. If H-bombs exist—and they do—some *man* controls them. In terms of morals *there is no such thing as 'state.'* Just men. Individuals. Each responsible for his own acts."

"Anybody need a refill?" I asked.

Nothing uses up alcohol faster than political argument. I sent for another bottle.

I did not take part. I was not dissatisfied back when we were "ground under Iron Heel of Authority." I cheated Authority and rest of time didn't think about it. Didn't think about getting rid of Authority—impossible. Go own way, mind own business, not be bothered—

True, didn't have luxuries then; by Earthside standards we were poor. If had to be imported, mostly did without; don't think there was a powered door in all Luna. Even p-suits used to be fetched up from Terra—until a smart Chinee before I was born figured how to make "monkey copies" better and simpler. (Could dump two Chinee down in one of our maria and they would get rich selling rocks to each other while raising twelve kids. Then a Hindu would sell retail stuff he got from them wholesale—below cost at fat profit. We got along.)

I had seen those luxuries Earthside. Wasn't worth what they put up with. Don't mean heavy gravity, that doesn't bother them; I mean nonsense. All time kukai moa. If chicken guano in one earthworm city were shipped to Luna, fertilizer problem would be solved for century. Do this. Don't do that. Stay back of line. Where's tax receipt? Fill out form. Let's see license. Submit six copies. Exit only. No left turn. No right turn. Queue up to pay fine. Take back and get stamped. Drop dead—but first get permit.

Wyoh plowed doggedly into Prof, certain she had all answers. But Prof was interested in questions rather than answers, which baffled her. Finally she said, "Professor, I can't understand you. I don't insist that you call it 'government'—I just want you to state what rules you think are necessary to insure equal freedom for all."

"Dear lady, I'll happily accept your rules."

"But you don't seem to want *any* rules!"

"True. But I will accept any rules that *you* feel necessary to *your* freedom. *I* am free, no matter what rules surround me. If I find them tolerable, I tolerate them; if I find them too obnoxious, I break them. I am free because I know that *I alone* am morally responsible for everything I do."

"You would not abide by a law that the majority felt was necessary?"

"Tell me what law, dear lady, and I will tell you whether I will obey it."

"You wiggled out. Every time I state a general principle, you wiggle out."

Prof clasped hands on chest. "Forgive me. Believe me, lovely Wyoming, I am most anxious to please you. You spoke of willingness to unite the front with anyone going your way. Is it enough that I want to see the Authority thrown off Luna . . . and would die to serve that end?"

Wyoh beamed. "It certainly is!" She fisted his ribs —gently—then put arm around him and kissed cheek. "Comrade! Let's get on with it!"

"Cheers!" I said. "Let's fin' Warden 'n' 'liminate him!" Seemed a good idea; I had had a short night and don't usually drink much.

Prof topped our glasses, held his high and announced with great dignity: "Comrades . . . *we declare the Revolution!*"

That got us both kissed. But sobered me, as Prof sat down and said, "The Emergency Committee of Free Luna is in session. We must plan action."

I said, "Wait, Prof! *I* didn't agree to anything. What's this 'Action' stuff?"

"We will now overthrow the Authority," he said blandly.

"*How?* Going to throw rocks at 'em?"

"That remains to be worked out. This is the planning stage."

I said, "Prof, you know me. If kicking out Authority was thing we could buy, I wouldn't worry about price."

" '—our lives, our fortunes, and our sacred honor.' "

"Huh?"

"A price that once was paid."

"Well—I'd go that high. But when I bet I want a chance to win. Told Wyoh last night I didn't object to long odds—"

" 'One in ten' is what you said, Mannie."

"Da, Wyoh. Show me those odds, I'll tap pot. But *can* you?"

"No, Manuel, I can't."

"Then why we talk-talk? *I* can't see *any* chance."

"Nor I, Manuel. But we approach it differently. Revolution is an art that I pursue rather than a goal I expect to achieve. Nor is this a source of dismay; a lost cause can be as spiritually satisfying as a victory."

"Not me. Sorry."

"Mannie," Wyoh said suddenly, "ask Mike."

I stared. "You serious?"

"Quite serious. If anyone can figure out odds, Mike should be able to. Don't you think?"

" 'Is that *all?*' My dear boy!"

"Prof, how many history books have you read?"

"I do not know. In excess of a thousand."

"Mike can zip through that many this afternoon, speed limited only by scanning method—he can store data much faster. Soon—minutes—he would have very fact correlated with everything else he knows, discrepancies noted, probability values assigned to uncertainties. Prof, Mike reads every word of every newspaper up from Terra. Reads all technical publications. Reads fiction—knows it's fiction—because isn't enough to keep him busy and is always hungry for more. If is any book he should read to solve this, say so. He can cram it down fast as I get it to him."

Prof blinked. "I stand corrected. Very well, let us see if he can cope with it. I still think there is something known as 'intuition' and 'human judgment.' "

"Mike has intuition," Wyoh said. "Feminine intuition, that is."

"As for 'human judgment,' " I added, "Mike isn't human. But all he knows he got from humans. Let's get you acquainted and you judge his judgment."

So I phoned. "Hi, Mike!"

"Hello, Man my only male friend. Greetings, Wyoh my only female friend. I heard a third person. I conjecture that it may be Professor Bernardo de la Paz."

Prof looked startled, then delighted. I said, "Too right, Mike. That's why I called you; Professor is not-stupid."

"Thank you, Man! Professor Bernardo de la Paz, I am delighted to meet you."

"I am delighted to meet you, too, sir." Prof hesitated, went on "Mi—Señor Holmes, may I ask how you knew that I was here?"

"I am sorry, sir; I cannot answer. Man? 'You know my methods.' "

"Mike is being crafty, Prof. It involves something he learned doing a confidential job for me. So he threw me a hint to let you think that he had identified you by hearing your presence—and he can indeed tell much from respiration and heartbeat . . . mass, approximate age, sex, and quite a bit about health; Mike's medical storage is as full as any other."

"I am happy to say," Mike added seriously, "that I detect no signs of cardiac or respiratory trouble, unusual for a man of the Professor's age who has spent so many years Earthside. I congratulate you, sir."

"Thank you, Señor Holmes."

"My pleasure, Professor Bernardo de la Paz."

"Once he knew your identity, he knew how old you are, when you were shipped and what for, anything that ever appeared about you in Lunatic or Moonglow or any Lunar publication, including pictures—your bank balance, whether you pay bills on time, and much more. Mike retrieved this in a split second once he had your name. What he didn't tell—because was my business—is that he knew I had invited you here, so it's a short jump to guess that you're still here when he heard heartbeat and breathing that matched you. Mike, no need to say 'Professor Bernardo de la Paz' each time; 'Professor' or 'Prof' is enough."

"Noted, Man. But he addressed me formally, with honorific."

"So both of you relax. Prof, you scan it? Mike knows much, doesn't tell all, knows when to keep mouth shut."

"I am impressed!"

"Mike is a fair dinkum thinkum—you'll see. Mike, I bet Professor three to two that Yankees would win pennant again. How chances?"

"I am sorry to hear it, Man. The correct odds, this early in the year and based on past performances of teams and players, are one to four point seven two the other way."

"Can't be that bad!"

"I'm sorry, Man. I will print out the calculations if you wish. But I recommend that you buy back your wager. The Yankees have a favorable chance to defeat any single team . . . but the combined chances of defeating all teams in the league, including such factors as weather, accidents, and other variables for the season ahead, place the club on the short end of the odds I gave you."

"Prof, want to sell that bet?"

"Certainly, Manuel."

"Price?"

"Three hundred Hong Kong dollars."

"You old thief!"

"Manuel, as you former teacher I would be false to you if I did not permit you to learn from mistakes. Señor Holmes—Mike my friend— May I call you 'friend'?"

"Please do." (Mike almost purred.)

"Mike amigo, do you also tout horse races?"

"I often calculate odds on horse races; the civil service computermen frequently program such requests. But the results are so at variance with expectations that I have concluded either that the data are too meager, or the horses or riders are not honest. Possibly all three. However, I can give you a formula which will pay a steady return if played consistently."

Prof looked eager. "What is it? May one ask?"

"One may. Bet the leading apprentice jockey to place. He is always given good mounts and they carry less weight. But don't bet him on the nose."

" 'Leading apprentice' . . . hmm. Manuel, do you have the correct time?"

"Prof, which do you want? Get a bet down before post time? Or settle what we set out to?"

"Unh, sorry. Please carry on. 'Leading apprentice—' "

"Mike, I gave you a recording last night." I leaned close to pickups and whispered: *"Bastille Day."*

"Retrieved, Man."

"Thought about it?"

"In many ways. Wyoh, you speak most dramatically."

"Thank you, Mike."

"Prof, can you get your mind off ponies?"

"Eh? Certainly, I am all ears."

"Then quit doing odds under your breath; Mike can do them faster."

"I was not wasting time; the financing of . . . joint ventures such as ours is always difficult. However, I shall table it; I am all attention."

"I want Mike to do a trial projection. Mike, in that recording, you heard Wyoh say we had to have free trade with Terra. You heard Prof say we should clamp an embargo on shipping food to Terra. Who's right?"

"Your question is indeterminate, Man."

"What did I leave out?"

"Shall I rephrase it, Man?"

"Sure. Give us discussion."

"In immediate terms Wyoh's proposal would be of great advantage to the people of Luna. The price of foodstuffs at catapult head would increase by a factor of at least four. This takes into account a slight rise in wholesale prices on Terra, 'slight' because the Authority now sells at approximately the free market price. This disregards subsidized, dumped, and donated foodstuffs, most of which come from the large profit caused by the controlled low price at catapult head. I will say no more about minor variables as they are swallowed by major ones. Let it stand that the immediate effect here would be a price increase of the close order of fourfold."

"Hear that, Professor?"

"Please, dear lady. I never disputed it."

"The profit increase to the grower is more than fourfold because, as Wyoh pointed out, he now must buy water and other items at controlled high prices. Assuming a free market throughout the sequence his profit enhancement will be of the close order of sixfold. But this would be offset by another factor: Higher prices for exports would cause higher prices for everything consumed in Luna, goods and labor. The total effect would be an enhanced standard of living for all on the close order of twofold. This would be accompanied by vigorous effort to drill and seal more farming tunnels, mine more ice, improve growing methods, all leading to greater export. However, the Terran Market is so large and food shortage so chronic that reduction in profit from increase of export is not a major factor."

Prof said, "But, Señor Mike, that would only hasten the day that Luna is exhausted!"

"The projection was specified as immediate, Señor Professor. Shall I continue in longer range on the basis of your remarks?"

"By all means!"

"Luna's mass to three significant figures is seven point three six times ten to the nineteenth power tonnes. Thus, holding other variables constant including Lunar and Terran populations, the present differential rate of export in tonnes could continue for seven point three six times ten to the twelfth years before using up one percent of Luna—round it as seven thousand billion years."

"What! Are you *sure?"*

"You are invited to check, Professor."

I said, "Mike, this a joke? If so, not funny even once!"

"It is not a joke, Man."

"Anyhow," Prof added, recovering, "it's not Luna's crust we are shipping. It's our lifeblood—water and organic matter. Not rock."

"I took that into consideration, Professor. This projection is based on controlled transmutation—any isotope into any other and postulating power for any reaction not exo-energetic. Rock *would* be shipped—transformed into wheat and beef and other foodstuffs."

"But we don't know how to do that! Amigo, this is ridiculous!"

"But we will know how to do it."

"Mike is right, Prof," I put in. "Sure, today we haven't a glimmer. But will. Mike, did you compute how many years till we have this? Might take a flier in stocks."

Mike answered in sad voice, "Man my only male friend save for the Professor whom I hope will be my friend, I tried. I failed. The question is indeterminate."

"Why?"

"Because it involves a break-through in theory. There is no way in all my data to predict when and where genius may appear."

Prof sighed. "Mike amigo, I don't know whether to be relieved or disappointed. Then that projection didn't mean anything?"

"Of course it meant something!" said Wyoh. "It means we'll dig it out when we need it. Tell him, Mike!"

"Wyoh, I am most sorry. Your assertion is, in effect, exactly what I was looking for. But the answer still remains: Genius is where you find it. No. I am so sorry."

I said, "Then Prof is right? When comes to placing bets?"

"One moment, Man. There is a special solution suggested by the Professor's speech last night—return shipping, tonne for tonne."

"Yes, but *can't* do that."

"If the cost is low enough, Terrans would do so. That can be achieved with only minor refinement, not a break-through, to wit, freight transportation up from Terra as cheap as catapulting down to Terra."

"You call this 'minor'?"

"I call it minor compared with the other problem, Man."

"Mike dear, how long? When do we get it?"

"Wyoh, a rough projection, based on poor data and largely intuitive, would be on the order of fifty years."

" 'Fifty years'? Why, that's nothing! We can have free trade."

"Wyoh, I said 'on the order of'—I did *not* say 'on the close order of.' "

"It makes a difference?"

"Does," I told her. "What Mike said was that he doesn't expect it sooner than five years but would be surprised if much longer than five hundred—eh, Mike?"

"Correct, Man."

"So need another projection. Prof pointed out that we ship water and organic matter and don't get it back—agree, Wyoh?"

"Oh, sure. I just don't think it's urgent. We'll solve it when we reach it."

"Okay, Mike—no cheap shipping, no transmutation: How long till trouble?"

"Seven years."

" 'Seven years!' " Wyoh jumped up, stared at phone. "Mike honey! You don't mean that?"

"Wyoh," he said plaintively, "I did my best. The problem has an indeterminately large number of variables. I ran several thousand solutions using many assumptions. The happiest answer came from assuming no increase in tonnage, no increase in Lunar population—restriction of births strongly enforced—and a greatly enhanced search for ice in order to maintain the water supply. That gave an answer of slightly over twenty years. All other answers were worse."

Wyoh, much sobered, said, "What happens in seven years?"

"The answer of seven years from now I reached by assuming the present situation, no change in Authority policy, and all major variables extrapolated from the empiricals implicit in their past behavior—a conservative answer of highest probability from available data. Twenty-eighty-two is the year I expect food riots. Cannibalism should not occur for at least two years thereafter."

" 'Cannibalism'!" She turned and buried head against Prof's chest.

He patted her, said gently, "I'm sorry, Wyoh. People do not realize how precarious our ecology is. Even so, it shocks *me*. I know water runs down hill . . . but didn't dream how terribly soon it will reach bottom."

She straightened up and face was calm. "Okay, Professor, I was wrong. Embargo it must be—and all that that implies. Let's get busy. Let's find out from Mike what our chances are. You trust him now—don't you?"

"Yes, dear lady, I do. We must have him on our side. Well, Manuel?"

Took time to impress Mike with how serious we were, make him understand that "jokes" could kill us (this machine who could not know human death) and to get assurance that he could and would protect secrets no matter what retrieval program was used—even our signals if not from us. Mike was hurt that I could doubt him but matter too serious to risk slip.

Then took two hours to program and re-program and change assumptions and investigate side issues before all four—Mike, Prof, Wyoh, self—were satisfied that we had defined it, i.e., what chance had revolution—*this* revolution, headed by us, success required before "Food Riots Day," against Authority with bare hands . . . against power of all Terra, all eleven billions, to beat us down and inflict their will—all with no rabbits out of hats, with certainty of betrayal and stupidity and faintheartedness, and fact that no one of us was genius, nor important in Lunar affairs. Prof made sure that Mike knew history, psychology, economics, name it. Toward end Mike was pointing out far more variables than Prof.

At last we agreed that programming was done—or that we could think of no other significant factor. Mike then said, "This is an indeterminate problem. How shall I solve it? Pessimistically? Or optimistically? Or a range of probabilities expressed as a curve, or several curves? Professor my friend?"

"Manuel?"

I said, "Mike, when I roll a die, it's one in six it turns ace. I don't ask shopkeeper to float it, nor do I caliper it, or worry about somebody blowing on it. Don't give happy answer, nor pessimistic; don't shove curves at us. Just tell in one sentence: What chances? Even? One in a thousand? None? Or whatever."

"Yes, Manuel Garcia O'Kelly my first male friend."

For thirteen and a half minutes was no sound, while Wyoh chewed knuckles. *Never* known Mike to take so long. Must have consulted every book he ever read and worn edges off random numbers. Was beginning to believe that he had been overloaded and either burnt out something or gone into cybernetic breakdown that requires computer equivalent of lobotomy to stop oscillations.

Finally he spoke. "Manuel my friend, I am terribly sorry!"

"What's trouble, Mike?"

"I have tried and tried, checked and checked. *There is but one chance in seven of winning!*"

7

I look at Wyoh, she looks at me; we laugh. I jump up and yip, "Hooray!" Wyoh starts to cry, throws arms around Prof, kisses him.

Mike said plaintively, "I do not understand. The chances are seven to one *against* us. Not *for* us."

Wyoh stopped slobbering Prof and said, "Hear that? Mike
75

said '*us*.' He included himself."

"Of course. Mike old cobber, we understood. But ever know a Loonie to refuse to bet when he stood a big fat chance of one in seven?"

"I have known only you three. Not sufficient data for a curve."

"Well . . . we're Loonies. Loonies bet. Hell, we *have* to! They shipped us up and bet us we couldn't stay alive. We fooled 'em. We'll fool 'em again! Wyoh. Where's your pouch? Get red hat. Put on Mike. Kiss him. Let's have a drink. One for Mike, too—want a drink, Mike?"

"I wish that I could have a drink," Mike answered wistfully, "as I have wondered about the subjective effect of ethanol on the human nervous system—I conjecture that it must be similar to a slight overvoltage. But since I cannot, please have one in my place."

"Program accepted. Running. Wyoh, where's *hat!*"

Phone was flat to wall, let into rock—no place to hang hat. So we placed it on writing shelf and toasted Mike and called him "Comrade!" and almost he cried. His voice fugged up. Then Wyoh borrowed Liberty Cap and put on me and kissed me into conspiracy, officially this time, and so all out that my eldest wife would faint did she see—then she took hat and put on Prof and gave him same treatment and I was glad Mike had reported his heart okay.

Then she put it on own head and went to phone, leaned close, mouth between binaurals and made kissing sounds. "That's for you, Mike dear comrade. Is Michelle there?"

Blimey if he didn't answer in soprano voice: "Right here, darling—and I am so '*appee!*"

So Michelle got a kiss, and I had to explain to Prof who "Michelle" was and introduce him. He was formal, sucking air and whistling and clasping hands—sometimes I think Prof was not right in his head.

Wyoh poured more vodka. Prof caught her, mixed ours with coffee, hers with chai, honey in all. "We have declared the Revolution," he said firmly, "now we execute it. With clear heads. Manuel, you were opted chairman. Shall we begin?"

"Mike is chairman," I said. "Obvious. Secretary, too. We'll never keep anything in writing; first security rule. With Mike, don't need to. Let's bat it around and see where we are; I'm new to business."

"And," said Prof, "still on the subject of security, the secret of Mike should be restricted to this executive cell, subject to unanimous agreement—all three of us—correction: all four of us—that is must be extended."

"What secret?" asked Wyoh. "Mike agreed to help our secrets. He's safer than we are; he can't be brainwashed. Can you be, Mike dear?"

"I could be brainwashed," Mike admitted, "by enough voltage. Or by being smashed, or subjected to solvents, or positive entropy through other means—I find the concept disturbing. But if by 'brainwashing' you mean could I be compelled to surrender our secrets, the answer is an unmodified negative."

I said, "Wye, Prof means secret of Mike *himself*. Mike old pal, you're our secret weapon—you know that, don't you?"

He answered self-consciously, "It was necessary to take that into consideration in computing the odds."

"How were odds without you, comrade? Bad?"

"They were not good. Not of the same order."

"Won't press you. But a secret weapon must be secret. Mike, does anybody else suspect that you are alive?"

"Am I alive?" His voice held tragic loneliness.

"Uh, won't argue semantics. Sure, you're alive!"

"I was not sure. It is good to be alive. No, Mannie my first friend, you three alone know it. My three friends."

"That's how must be if bet's to pay off. Is okay? Us three and never talk to anybody else?"

"But we'll talk to you lots!" Wyoh put in.

"It is not only okay," Mike said bluntly, "it is necessary. It was a factor in the odds."

"That settles it," I said. "They have everything else; we have Mike. We keep it that way. Say! Mike, I just had a horrid. We fight Terra?"

"We will fight Terra . . . unless we lose before that time."

"Uh, riddle this. Any computers smart as you? Any awake?"

He hesitated. "I don't know, Man."

"No data?"

"Insufficient data. I have watched for both factors, not only in technical journals but everywhere else. There are no computers on the market of my present capacity . . . but one of my model could be augmented just as I have been. Furthermore an experimental computer of great capacity might be classified and go unreported in the literature."

"Mmm . . . chance we have to take."

"Yes, Man."

"There aren't any computers as smart as Mike!" Wyoh said scornfully. "Don't be silly, Mannie."

"Wyoh, Man was not being silly. Man, I saw one disturbing

77

report. It was claimed that attempts are being made at the University of Peiping to combine computers with human brains to achieve massive capacity. A computing Cyborg."

"They say how?"

"The item was non-technical."

"Well . . . won't worry about what can't help. Right, Prof?"

"Correct, Manuel. A revolutionist must keep his mind free of worry or the pressure becomes intolerable."

"I don't believe a word of it," Wyoh added. "We've got Mike and we're going to win! Mike dear, you say we're going to fight Terra—and Mannie says that's one battle we can't win. You have some idea of how we can win, or you wouldn't have given us even one chance in seven. So what is it?"

"Throw rocks at them," Mike answered.

"Not funny," I told him. "Wyoh, don't borrow trouble. Haven't even settled how we leave this pooka without being nabbed. Mike, Prof says nine guards were killed last night and Wyoh says twenty-seven is whole bodyguard. Leaving eighteen. Do you know if that's true, do you know where they are and what they are up to? Can't put on a revolution if we dasn't stir out."

Prof interrupted. "That's a temporary exigency, Manuel, one we can cope with. The point Wyoming raised is basic and should be discussed. And daily, until solved. I am interested in Mike's thoughts."

"Okay, okay—but will you wait while Mike answers me?"

"Sorry, sir."

"Mike?"

"Mike?"

"Man, the official number of Warden's bodyguards is twenty-seven. If nine were killed the official number is now eighteen."

"You keep saying 'official number.' Why?"

"I have incomplete data which might be relevant. Let me state them before advancing even tentative conclusions. Nominally the Security Officer's department aside from clerks consists only of the bodyguard. But I handle payrolls for Authority Complex and twenty-seven is *not* the number of personnel charged against the Security Department."

Prof nodded. "Company spies."

"Hold it, Prof. Who are these other people?"

Mike answered, "They are simply account numbers, Man. I conjecture that the names they represent are in the Security Chief's data storage location."

"Wait, Mike. Security Chief Alvarez uses you for files?"

"I conjecture that to be true, since his storage location is under a locked retrieval signal."

I said, "Bloody," and added, "Prof, isn't that sweet? He uses Mike to keep records, Mike knows where they are—can't touch 'em!"

"Why not, Manuel?"

Tried to explain to Prof and Wyoh sorts of memory a thinkum has—permanent memories that can't be erased because patterns be logic itself, how it thinks; short-term memories used for current programs and then erased like memories which tell you whether you have honeyed coffee; temporary memories held long as necessary—milliseconds, days, years—but erased when no longer needed; permanently stored data like a human being's education—but learned perfectly and never forgotten—though may be condensed, rearranged, relocated, edited—and last but not finally, long lists of special memories ranging from memoranda files through very complex special programs, and each location tagged by own retrieval signal and locked or not, with endless possibilities on lock signals: sequential, parallel, temporal, situational, others.

Don't explain computers to laymen. Simpler to explain sex to a virgin. Wyoh couldn't see why, if Mike knew where Alvarez kept records, Mike didn't trot over and fetch.

I gave up. "Mike, can you explain?"

"I will try, Man. Wyoh, there is no way for me to retrieve locked data other than through external programming. I cannot program myself for such retrieval; my logic structure does not permit it. I must receive the signal as an external input."

"Well, for Bog's sake, what is this precious signal?"

"It is," Mike said simply, " 'Special File Zebra' "—and waited.

"Mike!" I said. "Unlock Special File Zebra." He did, and stuff started spilling out. Had to convince Wyoh that Mike hadn't been stubborn. He hadn't—he almost *begged* us to tickle him on that spot. Sure, he knew signal. Had to. But had to come from outside, that was how he was built.

"Mike, remind me to check with you all special-purpose locked-retrieval signals. May strike ice other places."

"So I conjectured, Man."

"Okay, we'll get to it later. Now back up and go over this stuff slowly—and, Mike, as you read out, store again, without erasing, under Bastille Day and tag it 'Fink File.' Okay?"

"Programmed and running."

"Do that with anything new he puts in, too."

Prime prize was list of names by warrens, some two hundred, each keyed with a code Mike identified with those blind pay accounts.

Mike read out Hong Kong Luna list and was hardly started when Wyoh gasped, "Stop, Mike! I've got to write these down!"

I said, "Hey! No writing! What's huhu?"

"That woman, Sylvia Chiang, is comrade secretary back home! But— But that means the Warden has our whole organization!"

"No, dear Wyoming," Prof corrected. "It means we have *his* organization."

"But—"

"I see what Prof means," I told her. *"Our* organization is just us three and Mike. Which Warden doesn't know. But now we know *his* organization. So shush and let Mike read. But don't write; you have this list—from Mike—anytime you phone him. Mike, note that Chiang woman is organization secretary, former organization, in Kongville."

"Noted."

Wyoh boiled over as she heard names of undercover finks in her town but limited herself to noting facts about ones she knew. Not all were "comrades" but enough that she stayed riled up. Novy Leningrad names didn't mean much to us; Prof recognized three, Wyoh one. When came Luna City Prof noted over half as being "comrades." I recognized several, not as fake subversives but as acquaintances. Not friends— Don't know what it would do to me to find someone I trusted on boss fink's payroll. But would shake me.

It shook Wyoh. When Mike finished she said, "I've got to get home! Never in my life have I helped eliminate anyone but I am going to *enjoy* putting the black on these spies!"

Prof said quietly, "No one will be eliminated, dear Wyoming."

"What? Professor, can't you take it? Though I've never killed anyone, I've always known it might have to be done."

He shook head. "Killing is not the way to handle a spy, not when he doesn't know that *you* know that he is a spy."

She blinked. "I must be dense."

"No, dear lady. Instead you have a charming honesty . . . a weakness you must guard against. The thing to do with a spy is to let him breathe, encyst him with loyal comrades, and feed him harmless information to please his employers. These creatures will be taken into our organization. Don't be shocked; they will be in very special cells. 'Cages' is a better word. But it would be the greatest waste to eliminate

80

them—not only would each spy be replaced with someone new but also killing these traitors would tell the Warden that we have penetrated his secrets. Mike amigo mio, there should be in that file a dossier on me. Will you see?"

Were long notes on Prof, and I was embarrassed as they added up to "harmless old fool." He was tagged as a subversive—that was why he had been sent to The Rock—as a member of underground group in Luna City. But was described as a "troublemaker" in organization, one who rarely agreed with others.

Prof dimpled and looked pleased. "I must consider trying to sell out and get myself placed on the Warden's payroll." Wyoh did not think this funny, especially when he made clear was not joke, merely unsure tactic was practical. "Revolutions must be financed, dear lady, and one way is for a revolutionary to become a police spy. It is probable that some of those prima-facie traitors are actually on our side."

"I wouldn't trust them!"

"Ah, yes, that is the rub with double agents, to be *certain* where their loyalties—if any—lie. Do you wish your own dossier? Or would you rather hear it in private?"

Wyoh's record showed no surprises. Warden's finks had tabbed her years back. But I was surprised that I had a record, too—routine check made when I was cleared to work in Authority Complex. Was classed as "non-political" and someone had added "not too bright" which was both unkind and true or why would I get mixed up in Revolution?

Prof had Mike stop read-out (hours more), leaned back and looked thoughtful. "One thing is clear," he said. "The Warden knew plenty about Wyoming and myself long ago. But you, Manuel, are not on his black list."

"After last night?"

"Ah, so. Mike, do you have *anything* in that file entered in the last twenty-four hours?"

Nothing. Prof said, "Wyoming is right that we cannot stay here forever. Manuel, how many names did you recognize? Six, was it? Did you see any of them last night?"

"No. But might have seen me."

"More likely they missed you in the crowd. I did not spot you until I came down front and I've known you since you were a boy. But it is most unlikely that Wyoming traveled from Hong Kong and spoke at the meeting without her activity being known to the Warden." He looked at Wyoh. "Dear lady, could you bring yourself to play the nominal role of an old man's folly?"

"I suppose so. How, Professor?"

"Manuel is probably in the clear. I am not but from my dossier it seems unlikely that the Authority's finks will bother to pick me up. You they may wish to question or even to hold; you are rated as dangerous. It would be wise for you to stay out of sight. This room— I'm thinking of renting it for a period—weeks or even years. You could hide in it—if you do not mind the obvious construction that would be placed on your staying here."

Wyoh chuckled. "Why, you darling! Do you think I care what anyone thinks? I'd be delighted to play the role of your bundle baby—and don't be too sure I'd be just playing."

"Never tease an old dog," he said mildly. "He might still have one bite. I may occupy that couch most nights. Manuel, I intend to resume my usual ways—and so should you. While I feel that it will take a busy cossack to arrest me, I will sleep sounder in this hideaway. But in addition to being a hideout this room is good for cell meetings; it has a phone."

Mike said, "Professor, may I offer a suggestion?"

"Certainly, amigo, we want your thoughts."

"I conclude that the hazards increase with each meeting of our executive cell. But meetings need not be corporal; you can meet—and I can join you if I am welcome—by phone."

"You are always welcome, Comrade Mike; we need you. However—" Prof looked worried.

I said, "Prof, don't worry about anybody listening in." I explained how to place a "Sherlock" call. "Phones are safe if Mike supervises call. Reminds me— You haven't been told how to reach Mike. How, Mike? Prof use my number?"

Between them, they settled on MYSTERIOUS. Prof and Mike shared childlike joy in intrigue for own sake. I suspect Prof enjoyed being rebel long before he worked out his political philosophy, while Mike—how could human freedom matter to him? Revolution was a game—a game that gave him companionship and chance to show off talents. Mike was as conceited a machine as you are ever likely to meet.

"But we still need this room," Prof said, reached into pouch, hauled out thick wad of bills.

I blinked. "Prof, robbed a bank?"

"Not recently. Perhaps again in the future of the Cause requires it. A rental period of one lunar should do as a starter. Will you arrange it, Manuel? The management might be surprised to hear my voice; I came in through a delivery door."

I called manager, bargained for dated key, four weeks. He

82

asked nine hundred Hong Kong. I offered nine hundred Authority. He wanted to know how many would use room? I asked if was policy of Raffles to snoop affairs of guests?

We settled at HK$475; I sent up bills, he sent down two dated keys. I gave one to Wyoh, one to Prof, kept one-day key, knowing they would not reset lock unless we failed to pay at end of lunar.

(Earthside I ran into insolent practice of requiring hotel guest to sign chop—even show identification!)

I asked, "What next? Food?"

"I'm not hungry, Mannie."

"Manuel, you asked us to wait while Mike settled your questions. Let's get back to the basic problem: how we are to cope when we find ourselves facing Terra, David facing Goliath."

"Oh. Been hoping that would go away. Mike? You really have ideas?"

"I *said* I did, Man," he answered plaintively. "We can throw rocks."

"Bog's sake! No time for jokes."

"But, Man," he protested, "we *can* throw rocks at Terra. We will."

8

Took time to get through my skull that Mike was serious, and scheme might work. Then took longer to show Wyoh and Prof how second part was true. Yet both parts should have been obvious.

Mike reasoned so: What is "war"? One book defined war as use of force to achieve political result. And "force" is action of one body on another applied by means of energy.

In war this is done by "weapons"—Luna had none. But weapons, when Mike examined them as class, turned out to be engines for manipulating energy—and energy Luna has plenty. Solar flux alone is good for around one kilowatt per square meter of surface at Lunar noon; sunpower, though cyclic, is effectively unlimited. Hydrogen fusion power is almost as unlimited and cheaper, once ice is mined, magnetic pinchbottle set up. Luna has energy—how to use?

But Luna also has energy of position; she sits at top of gravity well eleven kilometers per second deep and kept from falling in by curb only two and a half km/s high. Mike knew that curb; daily he tossed grain freighters over it, let them slide downhill to Terra.

Mike had computed what would happen if a freighter grossing 100 tonnes (or same mass of rock) falls to Terra, unbraked.

Kinetic energy as it hits is 6.25×10^{12} joules—over six trillion joules.

This converts in split second to heat. Explosion, big one!

Should been obvious. Look at Luna: What you see? Thousands on thousands of craters—places where Somebody got playful throwing rocks.

Wyoh said, "Joules don't mean much to me. How does that compare with H-bombs?"

"Uh—" I started to round off in head. Mike's "head" works faster; he answered, "The concussion of a hundred-tonne mass on Terra approaches the yield of a two-kilotonne atomic bomb."

" 'Kilo' is a thousand," Wyoh murmured, "and 'mega' is a million— Why, that's only one fifty-thousandth as much as a hundred-megatonne bomb. Wasn't that the size Sovunion used?"

"Wyoh, honey," I said gently, "that's not how it works. Turn it around. A two-kilotonne yield is equivalent to exploding two *million* kilograms of trinitrotoluol . . . and a kilo of TNT is quite an explosion— Ask any drillman. Two million kilos will wipe out good-sized town. Check, Mike?"

"Yes, Man. But, Wyoh my only female friend, there is another aspect. Multi-megatonne fusion bombs are inefficient. The explosion takes place in too small a space; most of it is wasted. While a hundred-megatonne bomb is rated as having fifty thousand times the yield of a two-kilotonne bomb, its destructive effect is only about thirteen hundred times as great as that of a two-kilotonne explosion."

"But it seems to me that thirteen hundred times is still quite a lot—if they are going to use bombs on us that much bigger."

"True, Wyoh my female friend . . . but Luna has *many* rocks."

"Oh. Yes, so we have."

"Comrades," said Prof, "this is outside my competence—in my younger or bomb-throwing days my experience was limited to something of the order of the one-kilogram chemical explosion of which you spoke, Manuel. But I assume that you two know what you are talking about."

"We do," Mike agreed.

"So I accept your figures. To bring it down to a scale that I can understand this plan requires that we capture the catapult. No?"

"Yes," Mike and I chorused.

"Not impossible. Then we must hold it and keep it operative. Mike, have you considered how your catapult can be protected against, let us say, one small H-tipped torpedo?"

Discussion went on and on. We stopped to eat—stopped business under Prof's rule. Instead Mike told jokes, each produced a that-reminds-me from Prof.

By time we left Raffles Hotel evening of 14th May '75 we had—Mike had, with help from Prof—outlined plan of Revolution, including major options at critical points.

When came time to go, me to home and Prof to evening class (if not arrested), then home for bath and clothes and necessities in case he returned that night, became clear Wyoh did not want to be alone in strange hotel—Wyoh was stout when bets were down, between times soft and vulnerable.

So I called Mum on a Sherlock and told her was bringing house guest home. Mum ran her job with style; any spouse could bring guest home for meal or year, and our second generation was almost as free but must ask. Don't know how other families work; we have customs firmed by a century; they suit us.

So Mum didn't ask name, age, sex, marital condition; was my right and she too proud to ask. All she said was: "That's nice, dear. Have you two had dinner? It's Tuesday, you know." "Tuesday" was to remind me that our family had eaten early because Greg preaches Tuesday evenings. But if guest had not eaten, dinner would be served—concession to guest, not to me, as with exception of Grandpaw we ate when was on table or scrounged standing up in pantry.

I assured her we had eaten and would make tall effort to be there before she needed to leave. Despite Loonie mixture of Muslims, Jews, Christians, Buddhists, and ninety-nine other flavors, I suppose Sunday is commonest day for church. But Greg belongs to sect which had calculated that sundown Tuesday to sundown Wednesday, local time Garden of Eden (zone minus-two, Terra) was *the* Sabbath. So we ate early in Terran north-hemisphere summer months.

Mum always went to hear Greg preach, so was not considerate to place duty on her that would clash. All of us went occasionally; I managed several times a year because terribly fond of Greg, who taught me one trade and helped me switch to another when I had to and would gladly have made it his arm rather than mine. But Mum always went—ritual not religion, for she admitted to me one night in pillow talk that she had no religion with a brand on it, then cautioned me not to tell Greg. I exacted same caution from her. I don't know Who is cranking; I'm pleased He doesn't stop.

But Greg was Mum's "boy husband," opted when she was very young, first wedding after her own—very sentimental about him, would deny fiercely if accused of loving him more than other husbands, yet took his faith when he was ordained and never missed a Tuesday.

She said, "Is it possible that your guest would wish to attend church?"

I said would see but anyhow we would rush, and said goodbye. Then banged on bathroom door and said, "Hurry with skin, Wyoh; we're short on minutes."

"One minute!" she called out. She's ungirlish girl; she appeared in one minute. "How do I look?" she asked. "Prof, will I pass?"

"Dear Wyoming, I am amazed. You were beautiful before, you are beautiful now—but utterly unrecognizable. You're safe—and I am relieved."

Then we waited for Prof to transform into old derelict; he would be it to his back corridor, then reappear as well-known teacher in front of class, to have witnesses in case a yellow boy was waiting to grab him.

It left a moment; I told Wyoh about Greg. She said, "Mannie, how good is this makeup? Would it pass in church? How bright are the lights?"

"No brighter than here. Good job, you'll get by. But do you want to go to church? Nobody pushing."

She thought. "It would please your moth—I mean, 'your senior wife,' would it not?"

I answered slowly, "Wyoh, religion is your pidgin. But since you ask . . . yes, nothing would start you better in Davis Family than going to church with Mum. I'll go if you do."

"I'll go. I thought your last name was 'O'Kelly'?"

"Is. Tack 'Davis' on with hyphen if want to be formal. Davis is First Husband, dead fifty years. Is family name and all our wives are 'Gospazha Davis' hyphenated with every male name in Davis line plus her family name. In practice Mum is only

'Gospazha Davis'—can call her that—and others use first name and add Davis if they write a cheque or something. Except that Ludmilla is 'Davis-Davis' because proud of double membership, birth and option."

"I see. Then if a man is 'John Davis,' he's a son, but if he has some other last name he's your co-husband. But a girl would be 'Jenny Davis' either way, wouldn't she? How do I tell? By her age? No, that wouldn't help. I'm confused! And I thought clan marriages were complex. Or polyandries—though mine wasn't; at least my husbands had the same last name."

"No trouble. When you hear a woman about forty address a fifteen-year-old as 'Mama Milla,' you'll know which is wife and which is daughter—not even that complex as we don't have daughters home past husband-high; they get opted. But might be visiting. Your husbands were named 'Knott'?"

"Oh, no, 'Fedoseev, Choy Lin and Choy Mu.' I took back my born name."

Out came Prof, cackled senilely (looked even worse than earlier!), we left by three exits, made rendezvous in main corridor, open formation. Wyoh and I did not walk together, as I might be nabbed; on other hand she did not know Luna City, a warren so complex even nativeborn get lost—so I led and she had to keep me in sight. Prof trailed to make sure she didn't lose me.

If I was picked up, Wyoh would find public phone, report to Mike, then return to hotel and wait for Prof. But I felt sure that any yellow jacket who arrested me would get a caress from number-seven arm.

No huhu. Up to level five and crosstown by Carver Causeway, up to level three and stop at Tube Station West to pick up arms and tool kit—but not p-suit; would not have been in character, I stored it there. One yellow uniform at station, showed no interest in me. South by well-lighted corridors until necessary to go outward to reach private easement lock thirteen to co-op pressure tunnel serving Davis Tunnels and a dozen other farms. I suppose Prof dropped off there but I never looked back.

I delayed locking through our door until Wyoh caught up, then soon was saying, "Mum, allow me to present Wyma Beth Johnson."

Mum took her in arms, kissed cheek, said, "So glad you could come, Wyma dear! Our house is yours!"

See why I love our old biddy? Could have quick-frosted Wyoh with same words—but was real and Wyoh knew.

Hadn't warned Wyoh about switch in names, thought of it

en route. Some of our kids were small and while they grew up despising Warden, no sense in risking prattle about "Wyoming Knott, who's visiting us"—that name was listed in "Special File Zebra."

So I missed warning her, was new to conspiracy.

But Wyoh caught cue and never bobbled.

Greg was in preaching clothes and would have to leave in minutes. Mum did not hurry, took Wyoh down line of husbands—Grandpaw, Greg, Hans—then up line of wives—Ludmilla, Lenore, Sidris, Anna—with stately grace, then started on our kids.

I said, "Mum? Excuse me, want to change arms." Her eyebrows went up a millimeter, meaning: "We'll speak of this but not in front of children"—so I added: "Know it's late, Greg's sneaking look at watch. And Wyma and I are going to church. So 'scuse, please."

She relaxed. "Certainly, dear." As she turned away I saw her arm go around Wyoh's waist, so I relaxed.

I changed arms, replacing number seven with social arm. But was excuse to duck into phone cupboard and punch "MYCROFTXXX." "Mike, we're home. But about to go to church. Don't think you can listen there, so I'll check in later. Heard from Prof?"

"Not yet, Man. Which church is it? I may have some circuit."

"Pillar of Fire Repentance Tabernacle—"

"No reference."

"Slow to my speed, pal. Meets in West-Three Community Hall. That's south of Station on Ring about number—"

"I have it. There's a pickup inside for channels and a phone in the corridor outside; I'll keep an ear on both."

"I don't expect trouble, Mike."

"It's what Professor said to do. He is reporting now. Do you wish to speak to him?"

"No time. 'Bye!"

That set pattern: Always keep touch with Mike, let him know where you are, where you plan to be; Mike would listen if he had nerve ends there. Discovery I made that morning, that Mike could listen at dead phone, suggested it—discovery bothered me; don't believe in magic. But on thinking I realized a phone could be switched on by central switching system without human intervention—if switching system had volition. Mike had bolshoyeh volition.

How Mike knew a phone was outside that hall is hard to say, since "space" could not mean to him what means to us.

But he carried in storage a "map"—structured relations—of Luna City's engineering, and could almost always fit what we said to what he knew as "Luna City"; hardly ever got lost.

So from day cabal started we kept touch with Mike and each other through his widespread nervous system. Won't mention again unless necessary.

Mum and Greg and Wyoh were waiting at outer door, Mum chomping but smiling. I saw she had lent Wyoh a stole; Mum was as easy about skin as any Loonie, nothing new-chummish—but church was another matter.

We made it, although Greg went straight to platform and we to seats. I settled in warm, mindless state, going through motions. But Wyoh did really listen to Greg's sermon and either knew our hymn book or was accomplished sight reader.

When we got home, young ones were in bed and most adults; Hans and Sidris were up and Sidris served cocoasoy and cookies, then all turned in. Mum assigned Wyoh a room in tunnel most of our kids lived in, one which had had two smaller boys last time I noticed. Did not ask how she had reshuffled, was clear she was giving my guest best we had, or would have put Wyoh with one of older girls.

I slept with Mum that night, partly because our senior wife is good for nerves—and nerve-racking things had happened—and partly so she would know I was *not* sneaking to Wyoh's room after things were quiet. My workshop, where I slept when slept alone, was just one bend from Wyoh's door. Mum was telling me, plain as print: "Go ahead, dear. Don't tell me if you wish to be mean about it. Sneak behind my back."

Which neither of us admitted. We visited as we got ready for bed, chatted after light out, then I turned over.

Instead of saying goodnight Mum said, "Manuel? Why does your sweet little guest make herself up as an Afro? I would think that her natural coloration would be more becoming. Not that she isn't perfectly charming the way she chooses to be."

So rolled over and faced her, and explained—sounded thin, so filled in. And found self telling all—except one point: Mike. I included Mike—but *not* as computer—instead as a man Mum was not likely to meet, for security reasons.

But telling Mum—taking her into my subcell, should say, to become leader of own cell in turn—taking Mum into conspiracy was not case of husband who can't keep from blurting everything to his wife. At most was hasty—but was best time if she was to be told.

Mum was smart. Also able executive; running big family

without baring teeth requires that. Was respected among farm families and throughout Luna City; she had been up longer than 90 percent. She could help.

And would be indispensable inside family. Without her help Wyoh and I would find it sticky to use phone together (hard to explain), keep kids from noticing (impossible!)—but with Mum's help would be no problems inside household.

She listened, sighed, said, "It sounds dangerous, dear."

"Is," I said. "Look, Mimi, if you don't want to tackle, say so . . . then forget what I've told."

"Manuel! Don't even say that. You are my husband, dear; I took you for better, for worse . . . and your wish is my command."

(My word, what a lie! But Mimi believed it.)

"I would not let you go into danger alone," she went on, "and besides—"

"What, Mimi?"

"I think every Loonie dreams of the day when we will be free. All but some poor spineless rats. I've never talked about it; there seemed to be no point and it's necessary to look up, not down, lift one's burden and go ahead. But I thank dear Bog that I have been permitted to live to see the time come, if indeed it has. Explain more about it. I am to find three others, is it? Three who can be trusted."

"Don't hurry. Move slowly. Be sure."

"Sidris can be trusted. She holds her tongue, that one."

"Don't think you should pick from family. Need to spread out. Don't rush."

"I shan't. We'll talk before I do anything. And Manuel, if you want my opinion—" She stopped.

"Always want your opinion, Mimi."

"Don't mention this to Grandpaw. He's forgetful these days and sometimes talkative. Now sleep, dear, and don't dream."

9

Followed a long time during which would have been possible to forget anything as unlikely as revolution had not details taken so much time. Our first purpose was not to be noticed. Long distance purpose was to make things as much worse as possible.

Yes, worse. Never was a time, even at last, when all Loonies wanted to throw off Authority, wanted it bad enough to revolt. All Loonies despised Warden and cheated Authority. Didn't mean they were ready to fight and die. If you had mentioned "patriotism" to a Loonie, he would have stared—or thought you were talking about his homeland. Were transported Frenchmen whose hearts belonged to "La Belle Patrie," ex-Germans loyal to Vaterland, Russkis who still loved Holy Mother Russia. But Luna? Luna was "The Rock," place of exile, not thing to love.

We were as non-political a people as history ever produced. I know, I was as numb to politics as any until circumstances pitched me into it. Wyoming was in it because she hated Authority for a personal reason, Prof because he despised all authority in a detached intellectual fashion, Mike because he was a bored and lonely machine and was for him "only game in town." You could not have accused us of patriotism. I came closest because I was third generation with total lack of affection for any place on Terra, had been there, disliked it and despised earthworms. Made me more "patriotic" than most!

Average Loonie was interested in beer, betting, women, and work, in that order. "Women" might be second place but first was unlikely, much as women were cherished. Loonies had learned there never were enough women to go around. Slow learners died, as even most possessive male can't stay alert every minute. As Prof says, a society adapts to fact, or doesn't survive. Loonies adapted to harsh facts—or failed and died. But "patriotism" was not necessary to survival.

Like old Chinee saying that "Fish aren't aware of water," I was not aware of any of this until I first went to Terra and even then did not realize what a blank spot was in Loonies under storage location marked "patriotism" until I took part in effort to stir them up. Wyoh and her comrades had tried to push "patriotism" button and got nowhere—years of work, a few thousand members, less than 1 percent and of that microscopic number almost 10 percent had been paid spies of boss fink!

Prof set us straight: Easier to get people to hate than to get them to love.

Luckily, Security Chief Alvarez gave us a hand. Those nine dead finks were replaced with ninety, for Authority was goaded into something it did reluctantly, namely spend money on us, and one folly led to another.

Warden's bodyguard had never been large even in earliest days Prison guards in historical meaning were unnecessary and that had been one attraction of penal colony system—cheap. Warden and his deputy had to be protected and visiting vips, but prison itself needed no guards. They even stopped guarding ships after became clear was not necessary, and in May 2075, bodyguard was down to its cheapest numbers, all of them new chum transportees.

But loss of nine in one night scared somebody. We knew it scared Alvarez; he filed copies of his demands for help in Zebra file and Mike read them. A lag who had been a police officer on Terra before his conviction and then a bodyguard all his years in Luna, Alvarez was probably most frightened and loneliest man in The Rock. He demanded more and tougher help, threatened to resign civil service job if he didn't get it—just a threat, which Authority would have known if it had really known Luna. If Alvarez had showed up in any warren as unarmed civilian, he would have stayed breathing only as long as not recognized.

He got his additional guards. We never found out who ordered that raid. Mort the Wart had never shown such tendencies, had been King Log throughout tenure. Perhaps Alvarez, having only recently succeeded to boss fink spot, wanted to make face—may have had ambition to be Warden. But likeliest theory is that Warden's reports on "subversive activities" cause Authority Earthside to order a cleanup.

One thumb-fingered mistake led to another. New bodyguards, instead of picked from new transportees, were elite convict troops, Federated Nations crack Peace Dragoons. Were mean and tough, did not want to go to Luna, and soon realized that "temporary police duty" was one-way trip. Hated

Luna and Loonies, and saw us as cause of it all.

Once Alvarez got them, he posted a twenty-four-hour watch at every interwarren tube station and instituted passports and passport control. Would have been illegal had there been laws in Luna, since 95 percent of us were theoretically free, either born free, or sentence completed. Percentage was higher in cities as undischarged transportees lived in barrack warrens at Complex and came into town only two days per lunar they had off work. If then, as they had no money, but you sometimes saw them wandering around, hoping somebody would buy a drink.

But passport system was not "illegal" as Warden's regulations were only written law. Was announced in papers, we were given week to get passports, and at eight hundred one morning was put in effect. Some Loonies hardly ever traveled; some traveled on business; some commuted from outlying warrens or even from Luna City to Novylen or other way. Good little boys filled out applications, paid fees, were photographed, got passes; I was good little boy on Prof's advice, paid for passport and added it to pass I carried to work in Complex.

Few good little boys! Loonies did not believe it. Passports? Whoever heard of such a thing?

Was a trooper at Tube Station South that morning dressed in bodyguard yellow rather than regimentals and looking like he hated it, and us. I was not going anywhere; I hung back and watched.

Novylen capsule was announced; crowd of thirty-odd headed for gate. Gospodin Yellow Jacket demanded passport of first to reach it. Loonie stopped to argue. Second one pushed past; guard turned and yelled—three or four more shoved past. Guard reached for sidearm; somebody grabbed his elbow, gun went off—not a laser, a slug gun, noisy.

Slug hit decking and went *whee-whee-hoo* off somewhere. I faded back. One man hurt—that guard. When first press of passengers had gone down ramp, he was on deck, not moving.

Nobody paid attention; they walked around or stepped over—except one woman carrying a baby, who stopped, kicked him carefully in face, then went down ramp. He may have been dead already, didn't wait to see. Understand body stayed there till relief arrived.

Next day was a half squad in that spot. Capsule for Novylen left empty.

It settled down. Those who had to travel got passports, diehards quit traveling. Guard at a tube gate became two men, one looked at passports while other stood back with gun drawn. One who checked passports did not try hard, which was well as most were counterfeit and early ones were crude. But before long, authentic paper was stolen and counterfeits were as dinkum as official ones—more expensive but Loonies preferred free-enterprise passports.

Our organization did not make counterfeits; we merely encouraged it—and knew who had them and who did not; Mike's records listed officially issued ones. This helped separate sheep from goats in files we were building—also stored in Mike but in "Bastille" location—as we figured a man with counterfeit passport was halfway to joining us. Word was passed down cells in our growing organization never to recruit anybody with a valid passport. If recruiter was not certain, just query upwards and answer came back.

But guards' troubles were not over. Does not help a guard's dignity nor add to peace of mind to have children stand in front of him, or behind out of eye which was worse, and ape every move he makes—or run back and forth screaming obscenities, jeering, making finger motions that are universal. At least guards took them as insults.

One guard back-handed a small boy, cost him some teeth. Result: two guards dead, one Loonie dead.

After that, guards ignored children.

We didn't have to work this up; we merely encouraged it. You wouldn't think that a sweet old lady like my senior wife would encourage children to misbehave. But she did.

Other things get single men a long way from home upset—and one we did start. These Peace Dragoons had been sent to The Rock without a comfort detachment.

Some of our fems were extremely beautiful and some started loitering around stations, dressed in less than usual—which could approach zero—and wearing more than usual amount of perfume, scents with range and striking power. They did not speak to yellow jackets nor look at them; they simply crossed their line of sight, undulating as only a Loonie gal can. (A female on Terra can't walk that way; she's tied down by six times too much weight.)

Such of course produces a male gallery, from men down to lads not yet pubescent—happy whistles and cheers for her beauty, nasty laughs at yellow boy. First girls to take this duty were slot-machine types but volunteers sprang up so fast that Prof decided we need not spend money. He was correct; even Ludmilla, shy as a kitten, wanted to try it and did not only because Mum told her not to. But Lenore, ten years older and prettiest of our family, did try it and Mum did not scold. She came back pink and excited and pleased with herself and anxious to tease enemy again. Her own idea; Lenore did not then know that revolution was brewing.

During this time I rarely saw Prof and never in public; we kept touch by phone. At first a bottleneck was that our farm had just one phone for twenty-five people, many of them youngsters who would tie up a phone for hours unless coerced. Mimi was strict; our kids were allowed one out-going call per day and max of ninety seconds on a call, with rising scale of punishment—tempered by her warmth in granting exceptions. But grants were accompanied by "Mum's Phone Lecture": "When I first came to Luna there were no private phones. You children don't know how soft . . . "

We were one of last prosperous families to install a phone; it was new in household when I was opted. We were prosperous because we never bought anything farm could produce. Mum disliked phone because rates to Luna City Co-op Comm Company were passed on in large measure to Authority. She never could understand why I could not ("Since you know all about such things, Manuel dear") steal phone service as easily as we liberated power. That a phone instrument was part of a switching system into which it must fit was no interest to her.

Steal it I did, eventually. Problem with illicit phone is how to receive incoming calls. Since phone is not listed, even if you tell persons from whom you want calls, switching system *itself* does not have you listed; is *no* signal that can tell it to connect other party with you.

Once Mike joined conspiracy, switching was no problem. I had in workshop most of what I needed; bought some items and liberated others. Drilled a tiny hole from workshop to phone cupboard and another to Wyoh's room—virgin rock a meter thick but a laser drill collimated to a thin pencil cuts rapidly. I unshipped listed phone, made a wireless coupling to line in its recess and concealed it. All else needed were binaural receptors and a speaker in Wyoh's room, concealed, and same in mine, and a circuit to raise frequency above audio to have silence on Davis phone line, and its converse to restore audio incoming.

Only problem was to do this without being seen, and Mum generaled that.

All else was Mike's problem. Used no switching arrangements; from then on used MYCROFTXXX only when calling from some other phone. Mike listened at all times in workshop and in Wyoh's room; if he heard my voice or hers say "Mike," he answered, but not to other voices. Voice patterns were as distinctive to him as fingerprints; he never made mistakes.

Minor flourishes—soundproofing Wyoh's door such as workshop door already had, switching to suppress my instrument or hers, signals to tell me she was alone in her room and door locked, and vice versa. All added up to safe means whereby Wyoh and I could talk with Mike or with each other, or could set up talk-talk of Mike, Wyoh, Prof, and self. Mike would call Prof wherever he was; Prof would talk or call back from a more private phone. Or might be Wyoh or myself had to be found. We all were careful to stay checked in with Mike.

My bootleg phone, though it had no way to punch a call, could be used to call any number in Luna—speak to Mike, ask for a Sherlock to anybody—not tell him number, Mike had all listings and could look up a number faster than I could.

We were beginning to see unlimited possibilities in a phone-switching system alive and on our side. I got from Mike and gave Mum still another null number to call Mike if she needed to reach me. She grew chummy with Mike while continuing to think he was a man. This spread through our family. One day as I returned home Sidris said, "Mannie darling, your friend with the nice voice called. Mike Holmes. Wants you to call back."

"Thanks, hon. Will."

"When are you going to invite him to dinner, Man? I think he's nice."

I told her Gospodin Holmes had bad breath, was covered with rank hair, and hated women.

She used a rude word, Mum not being in earshot. "You're afraid to let me see him. Afraid I'll opt out for him." I patted her and told her that was why. I told Mike and Prof about it. Mike flirted even more with my womenfolk after that; Prof was thoughtful.

I began to learn techniques of conspiracy and to appreciate Prof's feeling that revolution could be an art. Did not forget (nor ever doubt) Mike's prediction that Luna was only seven years from disaster. But did not think about it, thought about fascinating, finicky details.

Prof had emphasized that stickiest problems in conspiracy are communications and security, and had pointed out that they conflict—easier are communications, greater is risk to security; if security is tight, organization can be paralyzed by safety precautions. He had explained that cell system was a compromise.

I accepted cell system since was necessary to limit losses from spies. Even Wyoh admitted that organization without compartmentation could not work after he learned how rotten with spies old underground had been.

But I did not like clogged communications of cell system; like Terran dinosaurs of old, took too long to send message from head to tail, or back.

So talked with Mike.

We discarded many-linked channels I had suggested to Prof. We retained cells but based security and communication on marvelous possibilities of our dinkum thinkum.

Communications: We set up a ternary tree of "party" names:

Chairman, Gospodin Adam Selene (Mike)
Executive cell: Bork (me), Betty (Wyoh), Bill (Prof)
Bork's cell: Cassie (Mum), Colin, Chang
Betty's cell: Calvin (Greg), Cecilia (Sidris), Clayton
Bill's cell: Cornwall (Finn Nielsen), Carolyn, Cotter

—and so on. At seventh link George supervises Herbert, Henry, and Hallie. By time you reach that level you need 2,187 names with "H"—but turn it over to savvy computer who finds or invents them. Each recruit is given a party name and an emergency phone number. This number, instead of chasing through many links, connects with "Adam Selene," Mike.

Security: Based on double principle; no human being can be trusted with anything—but Mike could be trusted with everything.

Grim first half is beyond dispute. With drugs and other unsavory methods any man can be broken. Only defense is suicide, which may be impossible. Oh, are "hollow tooth" methods, classic and novel, some nearly infallible—Prof saw to it that Wyoh and myself were equipped. Never knew what he gave her as a final friend and since I never had to use mine, is no point in messy details. Nor am I sure I would ever suicide; am not stuff of martyrs.

But Mike could never need to suicide, could not be drugged, did not feel pain. He carried everything concerning us in a separate memory bank under a locked signal programmed *only* to our three voices, and, since flesh is weak, we added a signal under which any of us could lock out other two in emergency. In my opinion as best computerman in Luna, Mike could not remove this lock once it was set up. Best of all, nobody would ask master computer for this file because nobody knew it existed, did not suspect Mike-as-Mike existed. How secure can you be?

Only risk was that this awakened machine was whimsical.

Mike was always showing unforeseen potentials; conceivable he could figure way to get around block—if he wanted to.

But would never want to. He was loyal to me, first and oldest friend; he liked Prof; I think he loved Wyoh. No, no, sex meant nothing. But Wyoh is lovable and they hit it off from start.

I trusted Mike. In this life you have to bet; on that bet I would give any odds.

So we based security on trusting Mike with everything while each of us knew only what he had to know. Take that tree of names and numbers. I knew only party names of my cellmates and of three directly under me; was all I needed. Mike set up party names, assigned phone number to each, kept roster of real names versus party names. Let's say party member "Daniel" (whom I would not know, being a "D" two levels below me) recruits Fritz Schultz. Daniel reports fact but *not* name upwards; Adam Selene calls Daniel, assigns for Schultz party name "Embrook," then phones Schultz at number received from Daniel, gives Schultz his name Embrook and emergency phone number, this number being *different* for *each* recruit.

Not even Embrook's cell leader would know Embrook's emergency number. What you do not know you cannot spill, not under drugs nor torture, nor anything. Not even from carelessness.

Now let's suppose I need to reach Comrade Embrook. I don't know who he is; he may live in Hong Kong or be shopkeeper nearest my home. Instead of passing message down, hoping it will reach him, I call Mike. Mike connects me with Embrook at once, in a Sherlock, *without* giving me his number.

Or suppose I need to speak to comrade who is preparing cartoon we are about to distribute in every taproom in Luna. I don't know who he is. But I need to talk to him; something has come up.

I call Mike; Mike knows everything—and again I am quickly connected—and this comrade knows it's okay as Adam Selene arranged call. "Comrade Bork speaking"—and he doesn't know me but initial "B" tells him that I am vip indeed—"we have to change so-and-so. Tell your cell leader and have him check, but get on with it."

Minor flourishes—some comrades did not have phones; some could be reached only at certain hours; some outlying warrens did not have phone service. No matter, Mike knew everything—and rest of us did not know *anything* that could endanger any but that handful whom each knew face to face.

After we decided that Mike should talk voice-to-voice to an comrade under some circumstances, it was necessary to give him more voices and dress him up, make him three dimensions, create "Adam Selene, Chairman of the Provisional Committee of Free Luna."

Mike's need for more voices lay in fact that he had just one voder-vocoder, whereas his brain could handle a dozen conversations, or a hundred (don't know how many)—like a chess master playing fifty opponents, only more so.

This would cause a bottleneck as organization grew and Adam Selene was phoned oftener, and could be crucial if we lasted long enough to go into action.

Besides giving him more voices I wanted to silence one he had. One of those so-called computermen might walk into machines room while we were phoning Mike; bound to cause even his dim wit to wonder if he found master machine apparently talking to itself.

Voder-vocoder is very old device. Human voice is buzzes and hisses mixed various ways; true even of a coloratura soprano. A vocoder analyzes buzzes and hisses into patterns, one a computer (or trained eye) can read. A voder is a little box which can buzz and hiss and has controls to vary these elements to match those patterns. A human can "play" a voder, producing artificial speech; a properly programmed computer can do it as fast, as easily, as clearly as you can speak.

But voices on a phone wire are not sound waves but electrical signals; Mike did not need audio part of voder-vocoder to talk by phone. Sound waves were needed only by human at other end; no need for speech sounds inside Mike's room at Authority Complex, so I planned to remove them, and thereby any danger that somebody might notice.

First I worked at home, using number-three arm most of time. Result was very small box which sandwiched twenty voder-vocoder circuits minus audio side. Then I called Mike and told him to "get ill" in way that would annoy Warden. Then I waited.

We had done this "get ill" trick before. I went back to work once we learned that I was clear, which was Thursday that same week when Alvarez read into Zebra file an account of shambles at Stilyagi Hall. His version listed about one hundred people (out of perhaps three hundred); list included Shorty Mkrum, Wyoh, Prof, and Finn Nielsen but *not* me—apparently I was missed by his finks. It told how nine police officers, each deputized by Warden to preserve peace, had been shot down in cold blood. Also named three of our dead.

An add-on a week later stated that "the notorious agente provocateuse Wyoming Knott of Hong Kong in Luna, whose incendiary speech on Monday 13 May had incited the riot that cost the lives of nine brave officers, had not been apprehended in Luna City and had not returned to her usual haunts in Hong Kong in Luna, and was now believed to have died in the massacre she herself set off." This add-on admitted what earlier report failed to mention, i.e., bodies were missing and exact number of dead was not known.

This P.S. settled two things: Wyoh could not go home nor back to being a blonde.

Since I had not been spotted I resumed my public ways, took care of customers that week, bookkeeping machines and retrieval files at Carnegie Library, and spent time having Mike read out Zebra file and other special files, doing so in Room L of Raffles as I did not yet have my own phone. During that week Mike niggled at me like an impatient child (which he was), wanting to know when I was coming over to pick up more jokes. Failing that, he wanted to tell them by phone.

I got annoyed and had to remind myself that from Mike's viewpoint analyzing jokes was just as important as freeing Luna—and you *don't* break promises to a child.

Besides that, I got itchy wondering whether I could go inside Complex without being nabbed. We knew Prof was not clear, was sleeping in Raffles on that account. Yet they knew he had been at meeting and knew where he was, daily—but no attempt was made to pick him up. When we learned that attempt had been made to pick up Wyoh, I grew itchier. Was I clear? Or were they waiting to nab me quietly? Had to know.

So I called Mike and told him to have a tummyache. He did so, I was called in—no trouble. Aside from showing passport at station, then to a new guard at Complex, all was usual. I chatted with Mike, picked up one thousand jokes (with understanding that we would report a hundred at a time every three or four days, no faster), told him to get well, and went back to L-City, stopping on way out to bill Chief Engineer for working time, travel-and-tool time, materials, special service, anything I could load in.

Thereafter saw Mike about once a month. Was safe, never went there except when *they* called *me* for malfunction beyond ability of their staff—and I was always able to "repair" it, sometimes quickly, sometimes after a full day and many tests. Was careful to leave tool marks on cover plates, and had before-and-after print-outs of test runs to show what had been wrong, how I analyzed it, what I had done. Mike always worked perfectly after one of my visits; I was indispensable.

So, after I prepared his new voder-vocoder add-on, didn't hesitate to tell him to get "ill." Call came in thirty minutes. Mike had thought up a dandy; his "illness" was wild oscillations in conditioning Warden's residence. He was running its heat up, then down, on an eleven-minute cycle, while oscillating its air pressure on a short cycle, ca. 2c/s, enough to make a man dreadfully nervy and perhaps cause earache.

Conditioning a single residence should not go through a master computer! In Davis Tunnels we handled home and farm with idiot controls, feedbacks for each cubic with alarms so that somebody could climb out of bed and control by hand until trouble could be found. If cows got chilly, did not hurt corn; if lights failed over wheat, vegetables were okay. That Mike could raise hell with Warden's residence and nobody could figure out what to do shows silliness of piling everything into one computer.

Mike was happy-joyed. This was humor he really scanned. I enjoyed it, too, told him to go ahead, have fun—spread out tools, got out little black box.

And computerman-of-the-watch comes banging and ringing at door. I took my time answering and carried number-five arm in right hand with short wing bare; this makes some people sick and upsets almost everybody. "What in hell do *you* want, choom?" I inquired.

"Listen," he says, "Warden is raising hell! Haven't you found trouble?"

"My compliments to Warden and tell him I will override by hand to restore his precious comfort as soon as I locate faulty circuit—if not slowed up by silly questions. Are you going to stand with door open blowing dust into machines while I have cover plates off? If you do—since you're in charge—when dust puts machine on sputter, *you* can repair it. *I* won't leave a warm bed to help. You can tell that to your bloody Warden, too."

"Watch your language, cobber."

"Watch yours, convict. Are you going to close that door? Or shall I walk out and go back to L-City?" And raised number-five like a club.

He closed door. Had no interest in insulting poor sod. Was one small bit of policy to make everybody as unhappy as possible. He was finding working for Warden difficult; I wanted to make it unbearable.

"Shall I step it up?" Mike inquired.

"Um, hold it so for ten minutes, then stop abruptly. Then jog it for an hour, say with air pressure. Erratic but hard. Know what a sonic boom is?"

"Certainly. It is a—"

"Don't define. After you drop major effect, rattle his air ducts every few minutes with nearest to a boom system will produce. Then give him something to remember. Mmm . . . Mike, can you make his W.C. run backwards?"

"I surely can! All of them?"

"How many does he have?"

"Six."

"Well . . . program to give them all a push, enough to soak his rugs. But if you can spot one nearest his bedroom, fountain it clear to ceiling. Can?"

"Program set up!"

"Good. Now for your present, ducky." There was room in voder audio box to hide it and I spent forty minutes with number-three, getting it just so. We trial-checked through voder-vocoder, then I told him to call Wyoh and check each circuit.

For ten minutes was silence, which I spent putting tool markers on a cover plate which should have been removed had been anything wrong, putting tools away, putting number-six arm on, rolling up one thousand jokes waiting in print-out. I had found no need to cut out audio of voder; Mike had thought of it before I had and always chopped off any time door was touched. Since his reflexes were better than mine by a factor of at least a thousand, I forgot it.

At last he said, "All twenty circuits okay. I can switch circuits in the middle of a word and Wyoh can't detect discontinuity. And I called Prof and said Hello and talked to Mum on your home phone, all three at the same time."

"We're in business. What excuse you give Mum?"

"I asked her to have you call me, Adam Selene that is. Then we chatted. She's a charming conversationalist. We discussed Greg's sermon of last Tuesday."

"Huh? How?"

"I told her I had listened to it, Man, and quoted a poetic part."

"Oh, Mike!"

"It's okay, Man. I let her think that I sat in back, then slipped out during the closing hymn. She's not nosy; she knows that I don't want to be seen."

Mum is nosiest female in Luna. "Guess it's okay. But don't do it again. Um— *Do* do it again. You go to—you monitor—meetings and lectures and concerts and stuff."

"Unless some busybody switches me off by hand! Man, I can't control those spot pickups the way I do a phone."

"Too simple a switch. Brute muscle rather than solid-state flipflop."

"That's barbaric. And unfair."

"Mike, almost everything is unfair. What can't be cured—"

"—must be endured. That's a funny-once, Man."

"Sorry. Let's change it: What can't be cured should be tossed out and something better put in. Which we'll do. What chances last time you calculated?"

"Approximately one in nine, Man."

"Getting worse?"

"Man, they'll get worse for months. We haven't reached the crisis."

"With Yankees in cellar, too. Oh, well. Back to other matter. From now on, when you talk to anyone, if he's been to a lecture or whatever, you were there, too—and prove it, by recalling something."

"Noted. Why, Man?"

"Have you read 'The Scarlet Pimpernel'? May be in public library."

"Yes. Shall I read it back?"

"No, no! You're our Scarlet Pimpernel, our John Galt, our Swamp Fox, our man of mystery. You go everywhere, know everything, slip in and out of town without passport. You're always there, yet nobody catches sight of you."

His lights rippled, he gave a subdued chuckle. "That's fun, Man. Funny once, funny twice, maybe funny always."

"Funny always. How long ago did you stop gymkhana at Warden's?"

"Forty-three minutes ago except erratic booms."

"Bet his teeth ache! Give him fifteen minutes more. Then I'll report job completed."

"Noted. Wyoh sent you a message, Man. She said to remind you of Billy's birthday party."

"Oh, my word! Stop everything, I'm leaving. 'Bye!" I hurried out. Billy's mother is Anna. Probably her last—and right well she's done by us, eight kids, three still home. I try to be as careful as Mum never to show favoritism . . . but Billy is quite a boy and I taught him to read. Possible he looks like me.

Stopped at Chief Engineer's office to leave bill and demanded to see him. Was let in and he was in belligerent mood; Warden had been riding him. "Hold it," I told him. "My son's birthday and shan't be late. But must show you something."

Took an envelope from kit, dumped item on desk: corpse of house fly which I had charred with a hot wire and fetched. We do not tolerate flies in Davis Tunnels but sometimes one wanders in from city as locks are opened. This wound up in my workshop just when I needed it. "See that? Guess where I found it."

On that faked evidence I built a lecture on care of fine machines, talked about doors opened, complained about man on watch. "Dust can ruin a computer. *Insects* are unpardonable! Yet your watchstanders wander in and out as if tube station. Today both doors held open—while this idiot yammered. If I find more evidence that cover plates have been removed by hoof-handed choom who attracts flies—well, it's your plant, Chief. Got more than I can handle, been doing your chores because I like fine machines. Can't stand to see them abused! Good-bye."

"Hold on. I want to tell *you* something."

"Sorry, got to go. Take it or leave it, I'm no vermin exterminator; I'm a computerman."

Nothing frustrates a man so much as not letting him get in his say. With luck and help from Warden, Chief Engineer would have ulcers by Christmas.

Was late anyhow and made humble apology to Billy. Alvarez had thought up new wrinkle, close search on leaving Complex. I endured it with never a nasty word for Dragoons who searched me; wanted to get home. But those thousand jokes bothered them. "What's this?" one demanded.

"Computer paper," I said. "Test runs."

His mate joined him. Don't think they could read. They wanted to confiscate, so I demanded they call Chief Engineer. They let me go. I felt not displeased; more and more such and guards were daily more hated.

Decision to make Mike more a person arose from need to have any Party member phone him on occasion; my advice about concerts and plays was simply a side effect. Mike's voice over phone had odd quality I had not noticed during time I had visited him only at Complex. When you speak to a man by phone there is background noise. And you hear him breathe, hear heartbeats, body motions even though rarely conscious of these. Besides that, even if he speaks under a hush hood, noises get through, enough to "fill space," make him a body with surroundings.

With Mike was *none* of this.

By then Mike's voice was "human" in timbre and quality,

recognizable. He was baritone, had North American accent with Aussie overtones; as "Michelle" he (she?) had a light soprano with French flavor. Mike's personality grew also. When first I introduced him to Wyoh and Prof he sounded like a pedantic child; in short weeks he flowered until I visualized a man about own age.

His voice when he first woke was blurred and harsh, hardly understandable. Now it was clear and choice of words and phrasing was consistent—colloquial to me, scholarly to Prof, gallant to Wyoh, variation one expects of mature adults.

But background was dead. Thick silence.

So we filled it. Mike needed only hints. He did not make his breathing noisy, ordinarily you would not notice. But he would stick in touches. "Sorry, Mannie, you caught me bathing when the phone sounded"—and let one hear hurried breathing. Or "I was eating—had to swallow." He used such even on me, once he undertook to "be a human body."

We all put "Adam Selene" together, talking it over at Raffles. How old was he? What did he look like? Married? Where did he live? What work? What interests?

We decided that Adam was about forty, healthy, vigorous, well educated, interested in all arts and sciences and very well grounded in history, a match chess player but little time to play. He was married in commonest type, a troika in which he was senior husband—four children. Wife and junior husband not in politics, so far as we knew.

He was ruggedly handsome with wavy iron-gray hair and was mixed race, second generation one side, third on other. Was wealthy by Loonie standards, with interests in Novylen and Kongville as well as L-City. He kept offices in Luna City, outer office with a dozen people plus private office staffed by male deputy and female secretary.

Wyoh wanted to know was he bundling with secretary? I told her to switch off, was private. Wyoh said indignantly that she was not being snoopy—weren't we trying to create a rounded character?

We decided that offices were in Old Dome, third ramp, southside, heart of financial district. If you know L-City, you recall that in Old Dome some offices have windows since they can look out over floor of Dome; I wanted this for sound effects.

We drew a floor plan and had that office existed, it would have been between Aetna Luna and Greenberg & Co. I used pouch recorder to pick up sounds at spot; Mike added to it by listening at phones there.

Thereafter when you called Adam Selene, background was *not* dead. If "Ursula," his secretary, took call, it was: "Selene Associates. Luna shall be free!" Then she might say, "Will you hold? Gospodin Selene is on another call" whereupon you might hear sound of W.C., followed by running water and know that she had told little white lie. Or Adam might answer: "Adam Selene here. Free Luna. One second while I shut off the video." Or deputy might answer: "This is Albert Ginwallah, Adam Selene's confidential assistant. Free Luna. If it's a Party matter—as I assume it is; that was your Party name you gave—please don't hesitate; I handle such things for the Chairman."

Last was a trap, as every comrade was instructed to speak only to Adam Selene. No attempt was made to discipline one who took bait; instead his cell captain was warned that his comrade must not be trusted with anything vital.

We got echoes. "Free Luna!" or "Luna shall be free!" took hold among youngsters, then among solid citizens. First time I heard it in a business call I almost swallowed teeth. Then called Mike and asked if this person was Party member? Was not. So I recommended that Mike trace down Party tree and see if somebody could recruit him.

Most interesting echo was in File Zebra. "Adam Selene" appeared in boss fink's security file less than a lunar after we created him, with notation that this was a cover name for a leader in a new underground.

Alvarez's spies did a job on Adam Selene. Over course of months his File Zebra dossier built up: Male, 34-45, offices south face of Old Dome, usually there 0900-1800 Gr. except Saturday but calls are relayed at other hours, home inside urban pressure as travel time never exceeds seventeen minutes. Children in household. Activities include stock brokerage, farming interests. Attends theater, concerts, etc. Probably member Luna City Chess Club and Luna Assoc, d'Echecs. Plays ricochet and other heavy sports lunch hour, probably Luna City Athletic Club. Gourmet but watches weight. Remarkable memory plus mathematical ability. Executive type, able to reach decisions quickly.

One fink was convinced that he had talked to Adam between acts at revival of *Hamlet* by Civic Players; Alvarez noted description—and matched our picture all but wavy hair!

But thing that drove Alvarez crackers was that phone numbers for Adam were reported and every time they turned out wrong numbers. (Not nulls; we had run out and Mike was using any number not in use and switching numbers anytime new subscribers were assigned ones we had been using.) Alvarez tried to trace "Selene Associates" using a one-wrong-digit assumption—this we learned because Mike was keeping an ear on Alvarez's office phone and heard order. Mike used knowledge to play a Mikish prank: Subordinate who made one-changed-digit calls invariably reached Warden's private residence. So Alvarez was called in and chewed by Warden.

Couldn't scold Mike but did warn him it would alert any smart person to fact that somebody was playing tricks with computer. Mike answered that they were not that smart.

Main result of Alvarez's efforts was that each time he got a number for Adam we located a spy—a new spy, as those we had spotted earlier were never given phone numbers; instead they were recruited into a tail-chasing organization where they could inform on each other. But with Alvarez's help we spotted each new spy almost at once. I think Alvarez became unhappy over spies he was able to hire; two disappeared and our organization, then over six thousand, was never able to find them. Eliminated, I suppose, or died under questioning.

Selene Associates was not only phony company we set up. LuNoHoCo was much larger, just as phony, and not at all dummy; it had main offices in Hong Kong, branches in Novy Leningrad and Luna City, eventually employed hundreds of people most of whom were not Party members, and was our most difficult operation.

Mike's master plan listed a weary number of problems which *had* to be solved. One was finance. Another was how to protect catapult from space attack.

Prof considered robbing banks to solve first, gave it up reluctantly. But eventually we did rob banks, firms, and Authority itself. Mike thought of it. Mike and Prof worked it out. At first was not clear to Mike why we needed money. He knew as little about pressure that keeps humans scratching as he knew about sex; Mike handled millions of dollars and could not see any problem. He started by offering to issue an Authority cheque for whatever dollars we wanted.

Prof shied in horror. He then explained to Mike hazard in trying to cash a cheque for, let us say, AS$10,000,000 drawn on Authority.

So they undertook to do it, but retail, in many names and places all over Luna. Every bank, firm, shop, agency including Authority, for which Mike did accounting, was tapped for Party funds. Was a pyramided swindle based on fact, unknown to me but known to Prof and latent in Mike's immense knowledge, that most money is simply bookkeeping.

107

Example—multiply by hundreds of many types: My family son Sergei, eighteen and a Party member, is asked to start account at Commonwealth Shared Risk. He makes deposits and withdrawals. Small errors are made each time; he is credited with more than he deposits, is debited with less than he withdraws. A few months later he takes job out of town and transfers account to Tycho-Under Mutual; transferred funds are three times already-inflated amount. Most of this he soon draws out in cash and passes to his cell leader. Mike knows amount Sergei should hand over, but (since they do not know that Adam Selene and bank's computer-bookeeper are one and same) they have each been instructed to report transaction to Adam—keep them honest though scheme was not.

Multiply this theft of about HK$3,000 by hundreds somewhat like it.

I can't describe jiggery-pokery Mike used to balance his books while keeping thousands of thefts from showing. But bear in mind that an auditor must assume that machines are honest. He will make test runs to check that machines are working correctly—but will not occur to him that tests prove nothing because machine itself is dishonest. Mike's thefts were never large enough to disturb economy; like half-liter of blood, amount was too small to hurt donor. I can't make up mind who lost, money was swapped around so many ways. But scheme troubled me; I was brought up to be honest, except with Authority. Prof claimed that what was taking place was a mild inflation offset by fact that we plowed money back in—but I should remember that Mike had records and all could be restored after Revolution, with ease since we would no longer be bled in much larger amounts by Authority.

I told conscience to go to sleep. Was pipsqueak compared to swindles by every government throughout history in financing every war—and is not revolution a war?

This money, after passing through many hands (augmented by Mike each time), wound up as senior financing of LuNo-Ho Company. Was a mixed company, mutual and stock; "gentleman-adventurer" guarantors who backed stock put up that stolen money in own names. Won't discuss bookkeeping this firm used. Since Mike ran everything, was not corrupted by any tinge of honesty.

Nevertheless its shares were traded in Hong Kong Luna Exchange and listed in Zurich, London, and New York. *Wall Street Journal* called it "an attractive high-risk-high-gain investment with novel growth potential."

LuNoHoCo was an engineering and exploitation firm, engaged in many ventures, mostly legitimate. But prime purpose was to build a second catapult, secretly.

Operation could not be secret. You can't buy or build a hydrogen-fusion power plant for such and not have it noticed. (Sunpower was rejected for obvious reasons.) Parts were ordered from Pittsburgh, standard UnivCalif equipment, and we happily paid their royalties to get top quality. Can't build a stator for a kilometers-long induction field without having it noticed, either. But most important you cannot do major construction hiring many people and not have it show. Sure, catapults are mostly vacuum; stator rings aren't even close together at ejection end. But Authority's 3-g catapult was almost one hundred kilometers long. It was not only an astrogation landmark, on every Luna-jump chart, but was so big it could be photographed or seen by eye from Terra with not-large telescope. It showed up beautifully on a radar screen.

We were building a shorter catapult, a 10-g job, but even that was thirty kilometers long, too big to hide.

So we hid it by *Purloined Letter* method.

I used to question Mike's endless reading of fiction, wondering what notions he was getting. But turned out he got a better feeling for human life from stories than he had been able to garner from facts; fiction gave him a gestalt of life, one taken for granted by a human; he lives it. Besides this "humanizing" effect, Mike's substitute for experience, he got ideas from "not-true data" as he called fiction. How to hide a catapult he got from Edgar Allan Poe.

We hid it in literal sense, too; this catapult had to be underground, so that it would not show to eye or radar. But had to be hidden in more subtle sense; selenographic location had to be secret.

How can this be, with a monster that big, worked on by so many people? Put it this way: Suppose you live in Novylen; know where Luna City is? Why, on east edge of Mare Crisium; everybody knows that. So? What latitude and longitude? Huh? Look it up in a reference book! So? If you don't know *where* any better than that, how did you find it last week? No huhu, cobber; I took tube, changed at Torricelli, slept rest of way; finding it was capsule's worry.

See? You *don't know* where Luna City is! You simply get out when capsule pulls in at Tube Station South.

That's how we hid catapult.

Is in Mare Undarum area, "everybody knows that." But where it *is* and where we *said it was* differ by amount greater or less than one hundred kilometers in direction north, south, east, or west, or some combination.

Today you can look up its location in reference books—and find same wrong answer. Location of that catapult is still most closely guarded secret in Luna.

Can't be seen from space, by eye or radar. Is underground save for ejection and that is a big black shapeless hole like ten thousand others and high up an uninviting mountain with no place for a jump rocket to put down.

Nevertheless many people were there, during and after construction. Even Warden visited and my co-husband Greg showed him around. Warden went by mail rocket, commandeered for day, and his Cyborg was given coordinates and a radar beacon to home on—a spot in fact not far from site. But from there, was necessary to travel by rolligon and our lorries were not like passenger buses from Endsville to Beluthihatchie in old days; they were cargo carriers, no ports for sightseeing and a ride so rough that human cargo had to be strapped down. Warden wanted to ride up in cab but—sorry, Gospodin!—just space for wrangler and his helper and took both to keep her steady.

Three hours later he did not care about anything but getting home. He stayed one hour and was not interested in talk about purpose of all this drilling and value of resources uncovered.

Less important people, workmen and others, traveled by interconnecting ice-exploration bores, still easier way to get lost. If anybody carried an inertial pathfinder in his luggage, he could have located site—but security was tight. One did so and had accident with p-suit; his effects were returned to L-City and his pathfinder read what it should—i.e., what we *wanted* it to read, for I made hurried trip out with number-three arm along. You can reseal one without a trace if you do it in nitrogen atmosphere—I wore an oxygen mask at slight overpressure. No huhu.

We entertained vips from Earth, some high in Authority. They traveled easier underground route; I suppose Warden had warned them. But even on that route is one thirty-kilometer stretch by rolligon. We had one visitor from Earth who looked like trouble, a Dr. Dorian, physicist and engineer. Lorry tipped over—silly driver tried shortcut—they were not in line-of-sight for anything and their beacon was smashed. Poor Dr. Dorian spent seventy-two hours in an unsealed pumice igloo and had to be returned to L-City ill from hypoxia and overdose of radiation despite efforts on his behalf by two Party members driving him.

Might have been safe to let him see; he might not have spot-

110

ted doubletalk and would not have spotted error in location. Few people look at stars when p-suited even when Sun doesn't make it futile; still fewer can read stars—and nobody can locate himself on surface without help unless he has instruments, knows how to use them and has tables and something to give a time tick. Put at crudest level, minimum would be octant, tables, and good watch. Our visitors were even encouraged to go out on surface but if one had carried an octant or modern equivalent, might have had accident.

We did not make accidents for spies. We let them stay, worked them hard, and Mike read their reports. One reported that he was certain that we had found uranium ore, something unknown in Luna at that time, Project Centerbore being many years later. Next spy came out with kit of radiation counters. We made it easy for him to sneak them through bore.

By March '76 catapult was almost ready, lacking only installation of stator segments. Power plant was in and a co-ax had been strung underground with a line-of-sight link for that thirty kilometers. Crew was down to skeleton size, mostly Party members. But we kept one spy so that Alvarez could have regular reports—didn't want him to worry; it tended to make him suspicious. Instead we worried him in warrens.

10

Were changes in those eleven months. Wyoh was baptized into Greg's church, Prof's health became so shaky that he dropped teaching, Mike took up writing poetry. Yankees finished in cellar. Wouldn't have minded paying Prof if they had been nosed out, but from pennant to cellar in one season—I quit watching them on video.

Prof's illness was phony. He was in perfect shape for age, exercising in hotel room three hours each day, and sleeping in three hundred kilograms of lead pajamas. And so was I, and so was Wyoh, who hated it.

I don't think she ever cheated and spent night in comfort

though can't say for sure; I was not dossing with her. She had become a fixture in Davis family. Took her one day to go from "Gospazha Davis" to "Gospazha Mum," one more to reach "Mum" and now it might be "Mimi Mum" with arm around Mum's waist. When Zebra File showed she couldn't go back to Hong Kong, Sidris had taken Wyoh into her beauty shop after hours and done a job which left skin same dark shade but would not scrub off. Sidris also did a hairdo on Wyoh that left it black and looking as if unsuccessfully unkinked. Plus minor touches—opaque nail enamel, plastic inserts for cheeks and nostrils and of course she wore her dark-eyed contact lenses. When Sidris got through, Wyoh could have gone bundling without fretting about her disguise; was a perfect "colored" with ancestry to match—Tamil, a touch of Angola, German. I called her "Wyma" rather than "Wyoh."

She was gorgeous. When she undulated down a corridor, boys followed in swarms.

She started to learn farming from Greg but Mum put stop to that. While she was big and smart and willing, our farm is mostly a male operation—and Greg and Hans were not only male members of our family distracted; she cost more farming man-hours than her industry equaled. So Wyoh went back to housework, then Sidris took her into beauty shop as helper.

Prof played ponies with two accounts, betting one by Mike's "leading apprentice" system, other by his own "scientific" system. By July '75 he admitted that he knew nothing about horses and went solely to Mike's system, increasing bets and spreading them among many bookies. His winnings paid Party's expenses while Mike built swindle that financed catapult. But Prof lost interest in a sure thing and merely placed bets as Mike designated. He stopped reading pony journals—sad, something dies when an old horseplayer quits.

Ludmilla had a girl which they say is lucky in a first and which delighted me—every family needs a girl baby. Wyoh surprised our women by being expert in midwifery—and surprised them again that she knew nothing about baby care. Our two oldest sons found marriages at last and Teddy, thirteen, was opted out. Greg hired two lads from neighbor farms and, after six months of working and eating with us, both were opted in—not rushing things, we had known them and their families for years. It restored balance we had lacked since Ludmilla's opting and put stop to snide remarks from mothers of bachelors who had not found marriages—not that Mum wasn't capable of snubbing anyone she did not consider up to Davis standards.

Wyoh recruited Sidris; Sidris started own cell by recruiting her other assistant and Bon Ton Beauté Shoppe became hotbed of subversion. We started using our smallest kids for deliveries and other jobs a child can do—they can stake-out or trail a person through corridors better than an adult, and are not suspected. Sidris grabbed this notion and expanded it through women recruited in beauty parlor.

Soon she had so many kids on tap that we could keep all of Alvarez's spies under surveillance. With Mike able to listen at any phone and a child spotting it whenever a spy left home or place of work or wherever—with enough kids on call so that one could phone while another held down a new stake-out—we could keep a spy under tight observation and keep him from seeing anything we didn't want him to see. Shortly we were getting reports spies phoned in without waiting for Zebra File; it did a sod no good to phone from a taproom instead of home; with Baker Street Irregulars on job Mike was listening before he finished punching number.

These kids located Alvarez's deputy spy boss in L-City. We knew he had one because these finks did *not* report to Alvarez by phone, nor did it seem possible that Alvarez could have recruited them as none of them worked in Complex and Alvarez came inside Luna City only when an Earthside vip was so important as to rate a bodyguard commanded by Alvarez in person.

His deputy turned out to be two people—an old lag who ran a candy, news, and bookie counter in Old Dome and his son who was on civil service in Complex. Son carried reports in, so Mike had not been able to hear them.

We let them alone. But from then on we had fink field reports half a day sooner than Alvarez. This advantage—all due to kids as young as five or six—saved lives of seven comrades. All glory to Baker Street Irregulars!

Don't remember who named them but think it was Mike—I was merely a Sherlock Homes fan whereas he really did think he was Sherlock Holmes's brother Mycroft . . . nor would I swear he was not; "reality" is a slippery notion. Kids did not call themselves that; they had their own play gangs with own names. Nor were they burdened with secrets which could endanger them; Sidris left it to mothers to explain why they were being asked to do these jobs save that they were *never* to be told real reason. Kids will do anything mysterious and fun; look how many of their games are based on outsmarting.

Bon Ton salon was a clearinghouse of gossip—women get news faster than *Daily Lunatic*. I encouraged Wyoh to report to Mike each night, not try to thin gossip down to what seemed significant because was no telling what might be significant once Mike got through associating it with a million other facts.

Beauty parlor was also place to start rumors. Party had grown slowly at first, then rapidly as powers-of-three began to be felt and also because Peace Dragoons were nastier than older bodyguard. As numbers increased we shifted to high speed on agitprop, black-propaganda rumors, open subversion, provocateur activities, and sabotage. Finn Nielsen handled agitprop when it was simpler as well as dangerous job of continuing to front for and put cover-up activity into older, spy-ridden underground. But now a large chunk of agitprop and related work was given to Sidris.

Much involved distributing handbills and such. No subversive literature was ever in her shop, nor our home, nor that hotel room; distribution was done by kids, too young to read.

Sidris was also working a full day bending hair and such. About time she began to have too much to do I happened one evening to make walk-about on Causeway with Sidris on my arm when I caught sight of a familiar face and figure—skinny little girl, all angles, carrot-red hair. She was possibly twelve, at stage when a fem shoots up just before blossoming out into rounded softness. I knew her but could not say why or when or where.

I said, *"Psst,* doll baby. Eyeball young fem ahead. Orange hair, no cushions."

Sidris looked her over. "Darling, I knew you were eccentric. But she's still a boy."

"Damp it. Who?"

"Bog knows. Shall I sprag her?"

Suddenly I remembered like video coming on. And wished Wyoh were with me—but Wyoh and I were never together in public. This skinny redhead had been at meeting where Shorty was killed. She sat on floor against wall down front and listened with wide-eyed" seriousness and applauded fiercely. Than I had seen her at end in free trajectory—curled into ball in air and had hit a yellow jacket in knees, he whose jaw I broke a moment later.

Wyoh and I were alive and free because this kid moved fast in a crisis. "No, don't speak to her," I told Sidris. "But I want to keep her in sight. Wish we had one of your Irregulars here. Damn."

"Drop off and phone Wyoh, you'll have one in five minutes," my wife said.

I did. Then Sidris and I strolled, looking in shopwindows

and moving slowly, as quarry was window-shopping. In seven or eight minutes a small boy came toward us, stopped and said, "Hello, Auntie Mabel! Hi, Uncle Joe."

Sidris took his hand. "Hi, Tony. How's your mother, dear?"

"Just fine." He added in a whisper, "I'm Jock."

"Sorry." Sidris said quietly to me, "Stay on her," and took Jock into a tuck shop.

She came out and joined me. Jock followed her licking a lollipop. " 'Bye, Auntie Mabel! Thanks!" He danced away, rotating, wound up by that little redhead, stood and stared into a display, solemnly sucking his sweet. Sidris and I went home.

A report was waiting. "She went into Cradle Roll Crêche and hasn't come out. Do we stay on it?"

"A bit yet," I told Wyoh, and asked if she remembered this kid. She did, but had no idea who she might be. "You could ask Finn."

"Can do better." I called Mike.

Yes, Cradle Roll Crêche had a phone and Mike would listen. Took him twenty minutes to pick up enough to give analysis—many young voices and at such ages almost sexless. But presently he told me, "Man, I hear three voices that could match the age and physical type you described. However, two answer to names which I assume to be masculine. The third answers when anyone says 'Hazel'—which an older female voice does repeatedly. She seems to be Hazel's boss."

"Mike, look at old organization file. Check Hazels."

"Four Hazels," he answered at once, "and here she is: Hazel Meade, Young Comrades Auxiliary, address Cradle Roll Crêche, born 25 December 2063, mass thirty-nine kilos, height—"

"That's our little jump jet! Thanks, Mike. Wyoh, call off stake-out. Good job!"

"Mike, call Donna and pass the word, that's a dear."

I left it to girls to recruit Hazel Meade and did not eyeball her until Sidris moved her into our household two weeks later. But Wyoh volunteered a report before then; policy was involved. Sidris had filled her cell but wanted Hazel Meade. Besides this irregularity, Sidris was doubtful about recruiting a child. Policy was adults only, sixteen and up.

I took it to Adam Selene and executive cell. "As I see," I said, "this cells-of-three system is to serve us, not bind us. See nothing wrong in Comrade Cecilia having an extra. Nor any real danger to security."

"I agree," said Prof. "But I suggest that the extra member not be part of Cecilia's cell—she should not know the others, I

115

mean, unless the duties Cecilia gives her make it necessary. Nor do I think she should recruit, at her age. The real question is her age."

"Agreed," said Wyoh. "I want to talk about this kid's age."

"Friends," Mike said diffidently (diffidently first time in weeks; he was now that confident executive "Adam Selene" much more than lonely machine)—"perhaps I should have told you, but I have already granted similar variations. It did not seem to require discussion."

"It doesn't, Mike," Prof reassured him. "A chairman must use his own judgment. What is our largest cell?"

"Five. It is a double cell, three and two."

"No harm done. Dear Wyoh, does Sidris propose to make this child a full comrade? Let her know that we are committed to revolution . . . with all the bloodshed, disorder, and possible disaster that entails?"

"That's exactly what she is requesting."

"But, dear lady, while we are staking our lives, we are old enough to know it. For that, one should have an emotional grasp of death. Children seldom are able to realize that death will come to them personally. One might define adulthood as the age at which a person learns that he must die . . . and accepts his sentence undismayed."

"Prof," I said, "I know some mighty tall children. Seven to two some are in Party."

"No bet, cobber. It'll give odds that at least half of them don't qualify—and we may find it out the hard way at the end of this our folly."

"Prof," Wyoh insisted. "Mike, Mannie. Sidris is *certain* this child is an adult. And I think so, too."

"Man?" asked Mike.

"Let's find way for Prof to meet her and form own opinion. I was taken by her. Especially her go-to-hell fighting. Or would never have started it."

We adjourned and I heard no more. Hazel showed up at dinner shortly thereafter as Sidris' guest. She showed no sign of recognizing me, nor did I admit that I had ever seen her—but learned long after that she had recognized me, not just by left arm but because I had been hatted and kissed by tall blonde from Hong Kong. Furthermore Hazel had seen through Wyoming's disguise, recognized what Wyoh never did successfully disguise: her voice.

But Hazel used lip glue. If she ever assumed I was in conspiracy she never showed it.

Child's history explained her, far as background can explain steely character. Transported with parents as a baby much as Wyoh had been, she had lost father through accident while he was convict labor, which her mother blamed on indifference of Authority to safety of penal colonists. Her mother lasted till Hazel was five; what she died from Hazel did not know; she was then living in crèche where we found her. Nor did she know why parents had been shipped—possibly for subversion if they were both under sentence as Hazel thought. As may be, her mother left her a fierce hatred of Authority and Warden.

Family that ran Cradle Roll let her stay; Hazel was pinning diapers and washing dishes as soon as she could reach. She had taught herself to read, and could print letters but could not write. Her knowledge of math was only that ability to count money that children soak up through their skins.

Was fuss over her leaving crèche; owner and husbands claimed Hazel owed several years' service. Hazel solved it by walking out, leaving her clothes and fewer belongings behind. Mum was angry enough to want family to start trouble which could wind up in "brawling" she despised. But I told her privately that, as her cell leader, I did *not* want our family in public eye—and hauled out cash and told her Party would pay for clothes for Hazel. Mum refused money, called off a family meeting, took Hazel into town and was extravagant—for Mum—in re-outfitting her.

So we adopted Hazel. I understand that these days adopting a child involves red tape; in those days it was as simple as adopting a kitten.

Was more fuss when Mum started to place Hazel in school, which fitted neither what Sidris had in mind nor what Hazel had been led to expect as a Party member and comrade. Again I butted in and Mum gave in part way. Hazel was placed in a tutoring school close to Sidris' shop—that is, near easement lock thirteen; beauty parlor was by it (Sidris had good business because close enough that our water was piped in, and used without limit as return line took it back for salvage). Hazel studied mornings and helped in afternoons, pinning on gowns, handing out towels, giving rinses, learning trade—and whatever else Sidris wanted.

"Whatever else" was captain of Baker Street Irregulars.

Hazel had handled younger kids all her short life. They liked her; she could wheedle them into anything; she understood what they said when an adult would find it gibberish. She was a perfect bridge between Party and most junior auxiliary. She could make a game of chores we assigned and persuade them

117

to play by rules she gave them, and never let them know it was adult-serious—but child-serious, which is another matter.

For example:

Let's say a little one, too young to read, is caught with a stack of subversive literature—which happened more than once. Here's how it would go, after Hazel indoctrinated a kid:

ADULT: "Baby, where did you get this?"

BAKER STREET IRREGULAR: "I'm not a baby, I'm a big boy!"

ADULT: "Okay, big boy, where did you get this?"

B.S.I.: "Jackie give it to me."

ADULT: "Who is Jackie?"

B.S.I.: "Jackie."

ADULT: "But what's his last name?"

B.S.I.: "Who?"

ADULT: "Jackie."

B.S.I.: (scornfully) "Jackie's a girl!"

ADULT: "All right, where does she live?"

B.S.I.: "Who?"

And so on around— To all questions key answer was of pattern: "Jackie give it to me." Since Jackie didn't exist, he (she) didn't have a last name, a home address, nor fixed sex. Those children enjoyed making fools of adults, once they learned how easy it was.

At worst, literature was confiscated. Even a squad of Peace Dragoons thought twice before trying to "arrest" a small child. Yes, we were beginning to have squads of Dragoons inside Luna City, but never less than a squad—some had gone in singly and not come back.

When Mike started writing poetry I didn't know whether to laugh or cry. He wanted to publish it! Shows how thoroughly humanity had corrupted this innocent machine that he should wish to see his name in print.

I said, "Mike, for Bog's sake! Blown all circuits? Or planning to give us away?"

Before he could sulk Prof said, "Hold on, Manuel; I see possibilities. Mike, would it suit you to take a pen name?"

That's how "Simon Jester" was born. Mike picked it apparently by tossing random numbers. But he used another name for serious verse, his Party name, Adam Selene.

"Simon's" verse was doggerel, bawdy, subversive, ranging from poking fun at vips to savage attacks on Warden, system, Peace Dragoons, finks. You found it on walls of public W.C.s, or on scraps of paper left in tube capsules. Or in taprooms.

Wherever they were, they were signed "Simon Jester" and with a matchstick drawing of a little horned devil with big grin and forked tail. Sometimes he was stabbing a fat man with a pitchfork. Sometimes just his face would appear, big grin and horns, until shortly even horns and grin meant "Simon was here."

Simon appeared all over Luna same day and from then on never let up. Shortly he started receiving volunteer help; his verses and little pictures, so simple anybody could draw them, began appearing more places than we had planned. This wider coverage *had* to be from fellow travelers. Verses and cartoons started appearing inside Complex—which could *not* have been our work; we never recruited civil servants. Also, three days after initial appearance of a very rough limerick, one that implied that Warden's fatness derived from unsavory habits, this limerick popped up on pressure-sticky labels with cartoon improved so that fat victim flinching from Simon's pitchfork was recognizably Mort the Wart. *We* didn't buy them, *we* didn't print them. But they appeared in L-City and Novylen and Hong Kong, stuck almost everywhere—public phones, stanchions in corridors, pressure locks, ramp railings, other. I had a sample count made, fed it to Mike; he reported that over seventy thousand labels had been used in L-City alone.

I did not know of a printing plant in L-City willing to risk such a job and equipped for it. Began to wonder if might be another revolutionary cabal?

Simon's verses were such a success that he branched out as a poltergeist and neither Warden nor security chief was allowed to miss it. "Dear Mort the Wart," ran one letter. "Do please be careful from midnight to four hundred tomorrow. Love & Kisses, Simon"—with horns and grin. In same mail Alvarez received one reading: "Dear Pimplehead, If the Warden breaks his leg tomorrow night it will be *your* fault. Faithfully your conscience, Simon"—again with horns and smile.

We didn't have anything planned; we just wanted Mort and Alvarez to lose sleep—which they did, plus bodyguard. All Mike did was to call Warden's private phone at intervals from midnight to four hundred—an unlisted number supposedly known only to his personal staff. By calling members of his personal staff simultaneously and connecting them to Mort, Mike not only created confusion but got Warden angry at his assistants—he flatly refused to believe their denials.

But was luck that Warden, goaded too far, ran *down* a ramp. Even a new chum does that only once. So he walked on air and sprained an ankle—close enough to a broken leg and

Alvarez was there when it happened.

Those sleep-losers were mostly just that. Like rumor that Authority catapult had been mined and would be blown up, another night. Ninety plus eighteen men can't search a hundred kilometers of catapult in hours, especially when ninety are Peace Dragoons not used to p-suit work and hating it—this midnight came at new earth with Sun high; they were outside far longer than is healthy, managed to cook up their own accidents while almost cooking themselves, and showed nearest thing to mutiny in regiment's history. One accident was fatal. Did he fall or was he pushed? A sergeant.

Midnight alarums made Peace Dragoons on passport watch much taken by yawning and more bad-tempered, which produced more clashes with Loonies and still greater resentment both ways—so Simon increased pressure.

Adam Selene's verse was on a higher plane. Mike submitted it to Prof and accepted his literary judgment (good, I think) without resentment. Mike's scansion and rhyming were perfect, Mike being a computer with whole English language in his memory and able to search for a fitting word in microseconds. What was weak was self-criticism. That improved rapidly under Prof's stern editorship.

Adam Selene's by-line appeared first in dignified pages of *Moonglow* over a somber poem titled: "Home." Was dying thoughts of old transportee, his discovery as he is about to leave that Luna is his beloved home. Language was simple, rhyme scheme unforced, only thing faintly subversive was conclusion on part of dying man that even many wardens he has endured was not too high a price.

Doubt if *Moonglow's* editors thought twice. Was good stuff, they published.

Alvarez turned editorial office inside out trying to get a line back to Adam Selene. Issue had been on sale half a lunar before Alvarez noticed it, or had it called to his attention; we were fretted, we *wanted* that by-line noticed. We were much pleased with way Alvarez oscillated when he did see it.

Editors were unable to help fink boss. They told him truth: Poem had come in by mail. Did they have' it? Yes, surely . . . sorry, no envelope; they were never saved. After a long time Alvarez left, flanked by four Dragoons he had fetched along for his health.

Hope he enjoyed studying that sheet of paper. Was piece of Adam Selene's business stationery:

—and under that was typed *Home,* by Adam Selene, etc.

Any fingerprints were added after it left us. Had been typed on Underwood Office Electrostator, commonest model in Luna. Even so, were not too many as are importado; a scientific detective could have identified machine. Would have found it in Luna City office of Lunar Authority. Machines, should say, as we found six of model in office and used them in rotation, five words and move to next. Cost Wyoh and self sleep and too much risk even though Mike listened at every phone, ready to warn. Never did it that way again.

Alvarez was not a scientific detective.

11

In early '76 I had too much to do. Could not neglect customers. Party work took more time even though all possible was delegated. But decisions had to be made on endless things and messages passed up and down. Had to squeeze in hours of heavy exercise, wearing weights, and dasn't arrange permission to use centrifuge at Complex, one used by earthworm scientists to stretch time in Luna—while had used it before, this time could not advertise that I was getting in shape for Earthside.

Exercising without centrifuge is less efficient and was especially boring because did not know there would be need for it. But according to Mike 30 percent of ways events could fall required some Loonie, able to speak for Party, to make trip to Terra.

Could not see myself as an ambassador, don't have education and not diplomatic. Prof was obvious choice of those recruited or likely to be. But Prof was old, might not live to land Earthside. Mike told us that a man of Prof's age, body type, etc., had less than 40 percent chance of reaching Terra alive.

But Prof did gaily undertake strenuous training to let him make most of his poor chances, so what could I do but put on weights and get to work, ready to go and take his place if old heart clicked off? Wyoh did same, on assumption that something might keep me from going. She did it to share misery; Wyoh always used gallantry in place of logic.

On top of business, Party work, and exercise was farming. We had lost three sons by marriage while gaining two fine lads, Frank and Ali. Then Greg went to work for LuNoHoCo, as boss drillman on new catapult.

Was needful. Much skull sweat went into hiring construction crew. We could use non-Party men for most jobs, but key spots had to be Party men as competent as they were politically reliable. Greg did not want to go; our farm needed him and he did not like to leave his congregation. But accepted.

That made me again a valet, part time, to pigs and chickens. Hans is a good farmer, picked up load and worked enough for two men. But Greg had been farm manager ever since Grandpaw retired, new responsibility worried Hans. Should have been mine, being senior, but Hans was better farmer and closer to it; always been expected he would succeed Greg someday. So I backed him up by agreeing with his opinions and tried to be half a farm hand in hours I could squeeze. Left no time to scratch.

Late in February I was returning from long trip, Novylen, Tycho Under, Churchill. New tube had just been completed across Sinus Medii, so I went on to Hong Kong in Luna—business and did make contacts now that I could promise emergency service. Fact that Endsville-Beluthihatchie bus ran only during dark semi-lunar had made impossible before.

But business was cover for politics; liaison with Hong Kong had been thin. Wyoh had done well by phone; second member of her cell was an old comrade—"Comrade Clayton"—who not only had clean bill of health in Alverez's File Zebra but also stood high in Wyoh's estimation. Clayton was briefed on policies, warned of bad apples, encouraged to start cell system while leaving old organization untouched. Wyoh told him to keep his membership, as before.

But phone isn't face-to-face. Hong Kong should have been our stronghold. Was less tied to Authority as its utilities were not controlled from Complex; was less dependent because lack (until recently) of tube transport had made selling at catapult head less inviting; was stronger financially as Bank of Hong